The Last Voyage of the
Misty Day

The Last Voyage of the

Misty Day

Jackie French Koller

Atheneum   1992   New York

Maxwell Macmillan Canada
TORONTO
Maxwell Macmillan International
NEW YORK   OXFORD   SINGAPORE   SYDNEY

Atheneum
Macmillan Publishing Company
866 Third Avenue
New York, NY 10022

Maxwell Macmillan Canada, Inc.
1200 Eglinton Avenue East
Suite 200
Don Mills, Ontario M3C 3N1

Macmillan Publishing Company is part of the
Maxwell Communication Group of Companies.
First edition
Printed in the United States of America
10 9 8 7 6 5 4 3 2 1
The text of this book is set in 12 pt. Caledonia.
Design by Kimberly M. Adlerman

Library of Congress Cataloging-in-Publication Data

Koller, Jackie French.
The last voyage of the Misty Day/Jackie French Koller.
p.   cm.
Summary: Having reluctantly moved to Maine after her father's
death in Manhattan, fourteen-year-old Denise forges a healing
friendship with a boat owner surrounded by considerable mystery.
ISBN 0-689-31731-X
[1. Moving, Household—Fiction. 2. Maine—Fiction.] I. Title.
PZ7.K833Las 1992
[Fic]—dc20   91-17482

To Dad, my favorite old sailor

Chapter 1

Denny Townsend sat scrunched up in her seat with her cheek resting against the window as the bus bounced over the pothole-riddled roads, jarring her cheekbone. Her breath made one small, clear spot, surrounded by a steamy halo on the frosted glass. The rest of the bus was pandemonium as usual, with kids yelling, radios blaring, spitballs flying, smoke thick enough to cut.

"Somebody smoking back there?" the bus driver yelled, glowering at them all in his rearview mirror.

"Smoking? Back here?" An older kid in the seat next to Denny threw his cigarette on the floor and crushed it with his sneaker. Then he glanced at Denny. "Hey, yeah, it's the new freshman," he yelled. "Quit smokin', you. Don't they teach you no manners back in New *Yawk* City?"

Everybody around her laughed, but Denny just ignored them. The bus driver scowled. "I'm going to get you one of these days, Spence," he shouted.

"Me? Me?" the kid named Spence said, clutching his chest in feigned innocence. "What did I do?"

The bus driver shook his head and kept on driving.

At last the bus came to Denny's stop. She gathered up her books and squeezed past Spence, out into the aisle.

"You cut out that smokin' now," Spence yelled after her. "It's gonna stunt your growth." Another round of laughter broke out.

Denny stepped down from the bus, breathed deeply of the fresh salt air, and sighed. The wind was stiff and cold, and she put her book bag down for a minute, pulled on her hat and gloves, and zipped her coat all the way up. If the weather was like this in November, she thought, what was it going to be like by January?

She shouldered her bag again and started the long trek across the causeway that connected the mainland to Phinney's Island. It was still a mystery to her, why her mother had brought her here of all places, to this godforsaken lump of an island clinging by a string to the coast of Maine.

The wind filled her mouth and snatched her breath away, and she had to turn and struggle against it backward. She stared up at the sky. A gull stood out, hanging motionless, white against the clear blue.

"What—are you stupid?" she shouted. "What do you stay here for? Fly south, you dumb bird."

The gull paid her no mind, and she wondered how long it could float there like that without flapping a wing. As she neared the island the wind died a little, cut by the thick growth of pines and balsams that flanked the road. It pummeled her again full force, though, as she stepped out onto the bluff where the house stood. Denny struggled to pull the back storm door open, then wedged herself inside it while she fumbled with the key. The ancient lock grumbled and fought but finally gave way, and the wind-driven storm door shoved her through the open doorway and into the little kitchen.

It was almost as cold inside as out. Dropping her books on the kitchen table, Denny darted into the living room to turn up the heat, then stood over the single iron grate, letting the warm air pour over her.

She looked around the tiny room with its faded, peeling wallpaper, its spare, 1940s vintage furniture, and its ancient, blackened fireplace that belched smoke into the room anytime anyone was foolish enough to try and light it.

"Welcome home," she said to herself. Who would believe that less than a month ago she'd been living in a beautiful, luxury apartment on Ocean Parkway in Brooklyn?

At last the room warmed up enough for her to take off her coat. She flopped on the lumpy old couch and picked up her writing paper.

Dear Shell,

It isn't getting any better. Did I tell you the name of my school is Moose Hollow Regional Secondary School? (They pronounce it Moose Hollah.) Yeah, I guess I did. But did I tell you there's actually a moose head in the lobby! You have to see it to believe it. Everybody's into L. L. Bean clothes up here, the ones that can afford them, that is. You order them from a catalog that has a fish on the front! They wouldn't know a pair of Guess? jeans if they fell over them. When I first came here I used to try and dress nicely. I even wore what was left of my Benetton perfume. What a waste! Everybody up here smells like mosquito repellent.

Mom still cries every night in bed. She doesn't think I hear her, but I do. Write to me. I'm desperate!

Best friends forever,
Denny

Chapter 2

Denny saw the headlights swing into the driveway and she ran to open the kitchen door. Her mother fought her way around the storm door, trying to balance two sacks of groceries.

"Whew," she said, "windy, huh?"

Denny scowled. "Yeah," she said, "what else is new?"

Her mother lowered the groceries onto the kitchen table and walked into the living room.

"Nice and toasty in here, though," she called.

"Sure," Denny mumbled, "as long as you stay in the living room." She had never heard of a house with only one heat vent before.

"Well, I came up with a great idea how to fix that," her mother said, coming back out into the kitchen.

"Fix what?"

"The heat problem."

"You're going to fix the heat problem?" Denny had been a little skeptical of her mother's fix-it ideas ever since the night her mother had fixed the shower head drip by putting a balloon over the nozzle. Getting hit by a giant, ice-cold water balloon when she'd stepped, half-asleep, into the shower the next morning had not been Denny's idea of a swell way to start the day.

"Yup," answered her mother. She rummaged down into one of the grocery bags and pulled out a small, square box. Denny read the label.

"Ma," she said, "that's a fan."

"I know that," said her mother.

"Ma. Fans cool you down. How is a fan going to help our heat problem?"

"Fans don't just cool you down," said her mother. "They also move air. I'm going to clip this to the wall over the heat register, and when we're in the bedrooms or the bathroom we'll blow the warm air that way, and when we're in the kitchen we'll blow it this way, and when we're in the living room we'll just turn it off."

"The heat?"

"The fan, wise guy."

Denny shrugged. "Well," she said, "I guess it's worth a try."

"Sure it is," said her mother.

"Or we could just go back to New York where they have regular heat."

Her mother ignored her and went in to plug in the fan.

Denny unpacked the groceries and started putting them away.

"This must be one of the first refrigerators ever invented," she yelled, trying to cram a pint of ice cream into the tiny freezer. The freezer door wouldn't close. "It needs defrosting again."

Her mother came out and frowned. "Just take the ice cube trays out and make some more room. I don't have time to do it tonight."

"What's for dinner?"

"Fish."

"Again?"

"Fish is cheap up here, and it's good for you."

"I'm gonna turn into a seal," Denny complained.

Her mother disappeared into the living room again. "Want a fire?" she called.

"No, I didn't bring my gas mask."

"Very funny." Her mother returned a few minutes later, dressed in her jeans and fuzzy slippers. "I think it's warmer in here already," she said.

"Yeah, I'm starting to feel positively flushed," said Denny.

Her mother grinned at her wryly, then started rattling pots and pans. "Did you make any friends today?" she asked nonchalantly.

"No," said Denny, dropping down onto a kitchen chair, "did you?"

Her mother turned and put a hand on her hip. "Denny, I'm serious."

"So am I."

"Denny, I really don't think you're trying very hard."

Denny rolled her eyes up toward the ceiling. "I told you, Mom, these kids are weird. They don't speak the same language as me. They think a *block* is a chunk of ice."

"So learn their language. Is that so tough?"

"Ay-yuh."

Denny's mother sighed. "Denny, look. We're here and we're going to stay here, at least for a while anyway."

"But why?"

"You know why."

"Okay, so Daddy died. Does that have to change everything?"

Denny's mother turned abruptly back to the sink.

Denny sucked in a big breath of air and let it out slowly. "Okay, I'm sorry. I said the *D* word again. But you have to get used to it, Mom. You're not the only one who's hurting, you know."

Denny's mother sniffed, then turned and wiped her eyes with the kitchen towel. She walked over and sank down into the chair across the table from Denny. "You're right," she said. "I'm sorry."

Denny shook her head and picked at the plastic tablecloth. "I still can't believe there's no money," she mumbled.

Her mother stiffened. "Well, there isn't." She got up and marched back over to the sink.

"But how could he be so dumb? No savings, no insurance, nothing!"

"He didn't *plan* on dying at age thirty-six!"

"Well, he should've thought. You should've thought. You had a kid. Parents are supposed to think of these things."

Denny's mother whirled. There were tears in her eyes. "Is that all you care about?" she shouted. "Your cushy little life-style? What about your father? He's dead! Don't you care about that?"

"Of course I care!" Denny felt tears sting her eyes. She jumped up out of her chair, charged through the living room into her bedroom, and slammed the door. Immediately, the cold started creeping into her bones.

"Shoot!" she whispered under her breath. "You can't even sulk in your own room in this house." She put on her slippers, then pulled an old sweatshirt out of her closet and tossed it over her head. She went over to her window and leaned against it, rubbing a hole in the ice to look out of.

Marooned . . . that's what she was. All alone with a crazy woman on a stupid little iceberg in the North Atlantic. She scanned the dark horizon from the shore across the bay to Little Hog Island and out to the open sea—and then suddenly her attention darted back to Little Hog Island. Was that a light through the trees on the far side?

A shiver ran through her body. There was a story in town about Little Hog Island. Years ago the causeway used to go right through and connect the islands. A man named Rufus Day lived out on Little Hog Island. He was something of a hermit but pretty well off. He'd built himself a nice house on the bluff, and he had a big boat and his own marine railway for hauling it in and out of the water. In fifty-four, when the hurricane hit, Rufus Day refused to leave Little Hog Island. The road washed away, along with his house. Rufus and his boat, the *Misty Day*, disappeared too. Everyone figured they were all washed out to sea, but then one day, twenty years later, the *Misty Day* had suddenly reappeared overnight, hauled out and sitting on her cradle on Little Hog Island, just as nice as you please. Rumor had it that the boat had been found drifting somewhere, unmanned, and that some relative had had her brought back and hauled out, but townsfolk said the ghost of Rufus Day had sailed her all those long years and roamed her decks still, longing to take her to sea again. The *Misty Day* sat there yet, weathering in her cradle, and townsfolk kept a respectful distance.

As Denny stared, the light disappeared. She shivered again. Probably just a lobster boat going by, she told herself.

Chapter 3

Mrs. Townsend peeled back the layers of blankets and kissed Denny on the nose.

"I'm heading out," she said. "What are you going to do today?"

Denny resisted the urge to be sarcastic. Her mother's soft sobs had gone on longer than usual last night, and Denny knew their argument had hurt her. She felt bad too. She knew her mother was going through a tough time, having lost Denny's dad so unexpectedly and being forced to put her writing career on hold just when things were starting to look promising.

"Want to come into town with me?"

Denny shook her head. The *town* of Wellsley, Maine, consisted of the general store where her mother worked, the Congregational church, and a barn that served as the town hall, firehouse, and police station. "I've got a lot of homework," she said.

Her mother nodded. "I'll bring home a pizza," she said, "and we'll do something nice tonight, okay?"

"Like what?" said Denny.

"I don't know. Trivial Pursuit, maybe?"

Again, Denny resisted the urge to say, *Ooh,*

11

whoopee. Instead she just smiled and said, "That sounds nice."

Her mother ruffled her hair. "Go on back to sleep," she said. "No need to get up this early."

Denny pulled the quilt back around her and listened to the sound of the car engine fading into the distance. She was alone again. So alone. She wasn't used to being alone. No one was ever alone in New York City. She closed her eyes for a minute and pretended she was home. It was Saturday morning. She'd get up and watch cartoons for a while, then Shell would come over and they'd take the L up to Atlantic Avenue and do some shopping, maybe catch a movie. That evening Daddy might take her into Manhattan to see the Knicks play basketball. Daddy . . . Denny pressed her eyes tight against the tears. When would it stop hurting?

Outside her window she heard a long, low moan. It was the foghorn. She was used to it now. The beacon from the lighthouse didn't even keep her awake at night anymore. She got up, wrapped herself in her quilt, and made her way to the kitchen. She turned the oven on full blast and opened the door, letting the heat flood out into the little room. If her mother had been there, she would have yelled about wasting electricity.

Denny flipped on her radio/tape deck, the one modern convenience her mother had allowed her to bring. There was no TV, no VCR, no Nintendo, no compact disc player. There wasn't even a telephone. And Denny was only allowed to play the radio when her mother wasn't home. It was as if her mother was trying to pretend the world didn't exist anymore. Denny flipped the dial around. She got the farm news, the fishing report, the weather station, a bunch of country-western stations, and finally picked up a quasi-rock station out of Bangor that faded in and out. How she missed WFMU in New York.

Denny made some tea, got out a box of the powdery, dry, prepackaged orbs that passed for doughnuts in Wellsley, then pulled a chair over and ate with her feet propped up on the oven door.

What *was* she going to do all day? she wondered. The choices were not mind-boggling. She could a) study, b) read, c) write another letter to Shell, d) take a walk, or e) all of the above. She opted for e) but decided to start the day off with the walk since she couldn't stand being cooped up inside the dingy little cottage another minute. She dressed without even showering (who did she need to be clean for anyway?) and went outside.

It was eerie out there. A warm front had come in during the night and brought with it a thick fog, but now the fog had burned off the island, and the sun shone down brightly. All around the island, though, the fog still clung to the sea and the bay, so as Denny looked out, the island seemed adrift on a cloud. She walked to the edge of the bluff, where someone had long ago built an old concrete pier that jutted out high over the rocks. She leaned on the railing and stared as hard as she could into the swirling mist, but she could see nothing beyond her hand. She could hear the sea below, rolling and crashing, rolling and crashing, but she could not see it. It gave her a strange, giddy, floating feeling. Overhead, a gull glided by and disappeared into the mist. Denny leaned out over the sea, the railing supporting her waist, and lifted her arms like the gull's wings. Gracefully she waved them up and down, up and down, and for a moment she almost believed she was flying.

Chapter 4

Denny put the flag up on the mailbox and started back over the causeway again. The mist had cleared out completely now, and it was a beautiful day. Back in Brooklyn she would have been shivering, but here it felt like Indian summer. From this angle, Phinney's Island and Little Hog Island ran together and took on the shape of a rat lying on the water, the head being Little Hog Island, the body being Phinney's, and the long, skinny tail being the causeway that curved back to meet Denny. The sky above the islands was crystal clear, except for . . . except for *two* thin lines of smoke?

Denny blinked her eyes and stared again. The one line, the one above Phinney's, was from the cottage chimney, of course. But what was the second, the one that seemed to rise from the nose of the rat? Suddenly she remembered the light she had seen last night. There was someone out there, then; but doing what? Camping? This time of year? She looked at the shore. The tide was on its way out. If she hurried, she might be able to get over the bar and have time to investigate and get back again before the tide returned.

Denny was out of breath by the time she reached the end of the road. It gave her goose bumps again, the way the road went right on past the cottage, then ended abruptly at the edge of the water above the sandbar, or to be more specific, rockbar. Sand seemed to be a scarce commodity on the shores of Maine.

The water still lapped over the sandbar, and Denny sat down to wait for it to recede a little more. A high-pitched whine came to her, carried on the breeze from the same direction as the smoke. It did not seem an unearthly sound, but she began to have second thoughts about approaching whatever waited over there. Maybe she should wait and tell her mother. But then she knew she couldn't wait. The intrigue was too strong, and the promise of adventure too intoxicating. She would be careful and keep herself out of sight.

As soon as the larger rocks poked out of the water, Denny hopped from rock to rock across the bar. Little Hog Island, like Phinney's, turned a high, rocky shoulder to the sea, but sloped more gracefully toward the mainland. The shore side was easier walking, but the rocky side, thick with pines, provided better cover, so this was the route Denny chose. The island was small, probably no more than a quarter mile across, but the trees grew so densely that Denny was forced out onto the rocky crags, where the going was slow.

The whining grew louder as Denny drew closer to the plume of smoke. Soon the source was directly ahead, just below the bluffs. Denny knelt behind a scrub pine and parted the underbrush for a better look. What she saw made her catch her breath. The smoke was coming out of a small smokestack on the *Misty Day!*

Denny's heart pounded and her breath came in short puffs, but she resisted the temptation to run.

"It's real smoke," she told herself. "Ghosts don't play with fire."

As she watched, the whine suddenly stopped and a gray-bearded man appeared on the deck of the *Misty Day*. He wore a sailor's cap and puffed on a pipe, and as he stood staring out to sea he looked for all the world like the personification of the Ancient Mariner.

Her heart started to pound again. "He's real," she tried to convince herself. "He's perfectly real."

Then she wasn't so sure. Besides, the tide had turned and she wasn't sure how long it would take for the bar to be submerged again. She turned to go, when suddenly a strange little creature charged out of the bushes, snarling and snapping at her legs.

Denny screamed.

Chapter 5

Denny clapped a hand over her mouth, but it was too late. The man on the *Misty Day* turned immediately and stared straight at her.

"Who's that?" he yelled. "Who's up there!"

Denny was still trying to pull her leg away from the crazy little dog that had a fierce grip on her sock.

"Call your dog off," she shouted.

The man had climbed down out of the boat and was making his way up the hill.

"Marty!" he shouted. "Marty, cut that out."

Marty paid no attention whatsoever and went right on wrestling ferociously with Denny's leg. The more she shook it and kicked, the wilder he became, until she was really scared.

"Get him off me!" she shrieked. "He's going to rip my leg off."

The man finally made it up the hill and grabbed hold of the dog. He had to whack him repeatedly on his pushed-in little nose to get him to let go of the sock, and even after finally letting go, the dog kept on snarling and yapping.

Denny bent down and rubbed her ankle.

"What the heck is he, a pit bull?" she asked sullenly.

The man shook his head. "Just a pug with big ideas," he said. He put the dog down and gave him a gentle kick in the direction of the boat. "Go on, Marty. Get home," he said. Then he turned back to Denny. "You okay?"

Denny nodded. She eyed the dog warily as it wiggled its way down the bank, barely visible above the brush. "That's the ugliest dog I ever saw," she said.

The man laughed. "He's not much of a looker, that's true," he said, "but he's a good friend and a pretty fair watchdog." He looked at Denny pointedly when he said "watchdog." "Now, how about telling me who you are and what business you have on this island?"

Denny looked at him. "Me?" she said. "I'm not the one poking around the old ghost ship. I came here to see who you were."

The man laughed again. "Ghost ship?" he said. "What ghost ship? That's my boat. In fact I own this whole island, so I figure you're trespassing."

Denny stared at him in astonishment. She did some quick figuring in her head. She thought she'd heard somewhere that Rufus Day was in his sixties when the hurricane hit. That would make him close to a hundred by now, if he was still alive. This man was old but not ancient, maybe seventy-five at the most. Then again, maybe she'd heard wrong.

"Are you Rufus Day?" she asked.

The man raised an eyebrow. "Who?"

"Rufus Day owns this island, at least he did when he was alive . . . that is, if he's dead, I mean."

The old man lifted his cap and scratched a small bald spot on the top of his head. "You're not making much sense . . . uh, what's your name?"

"Denny."

The old man nodded as if her name confirmed something he had suspected. "Well, Denny, you're not making much sense, son. I don't much care who owned this island in the past. I own it now, and I want to know what you're doing on it."

Denny bristled. With her short hair and boyish name she was used to being taken for a boy, but she'd finally begun to develop and she had hoped that her gender was getting more evident.

"I'm not your *son*," she snapped, "and if it's any of your business, my mom and I are renting the Tucker place over on Phinney's for the winter."

The old man wrinkled his brow and nodded. "Ah," he said. "Thought the place looked occupied when I came by yesterday."

"Came by?" said Denny. "What do you mean, came by?"

"Drove by," the man said. "That's how I get out here. He pointed to a Jeep parked on the beach down below the bluff on the left. "My deed gives me the right to used the causeway."

"But the causeway is washed out," said Denny.

"The Jeep can still make it at low tide. I just have to time my comings and goings, that's all."

"What do you come out here for?" asked Denny.

"I live out here."

"Live out here? Where?"

"On the boat."

Denny wrinkled up her nose and stared at the *Misty Day*, perched up on her cradle, all weather-beaten and gray. "Live *there*?" she said. "Is that legal?"

The old man threw his head back and laughed again.

"Maybe not in New York where you come from," he said, "but the nice thing about Maine is folks mind their own business. You don't bother them, they don't bother you."

Denny's mouth dropped open. "How'd you know where I came from?" she asked.

"Your accent is a dead giveaway."

"*My* accent!" said Denny. "I don't have an accent. I talk normally. Everybody else around here has an accent." Then she hesitated. "Except you," she added. "You're not a Mainiac, are you?"

"No sir, not by either definition of the word. I'm just a retired engineer from Connecticut."

"Engineer as in train?" asked Denny, her interest piqued.

"No. Engineer as in electrical."

"Oh," said Denny. "So why live on an old boat? And why here? Why not Florida, where it's warm?"

The old man seemed suddenly impatient. He looked at his watch. "Haven't you got a tide to catch or something?"

"Oh, my gosh!" said Denny. "I forgot."

21

She started to dash off along the bluff the way she'd come.

"Easier walking down along the beach," said the old man.

"Oh, yeah," said Denny. "Thanks."

She started sliding down the bank, but the little dog came running up toward her again. The old man hurried down, cut in front of her, and scooped him up.

"Come on, Marty," he said. "I don't need any more protecting just now." He carried the dog off toward the boat.

"Hey," shouted Denny.

The old man looked over his shoulder. "Yeah?"

"What's your name?"

The man hesitated. "Jones," he said. "Mr. Jones."

Denny looked at him skeptically.

"Oh, and Dennis," he said, "you better tell your mom about me. Don't want to scare her someday when I'm driving by."

Denny threw her head up and stuck her chest out. "It's *Denise*," she said, and flounced off across the beach.

Chapter 6

"What city is served by Stapleton International Airport?" asked Denny's mother, "Dallas, Denver, or Detroit?"

"Denver," said Denny.

Her mother turned over the Trivial Pursuit card. "That's right. How did you know that?"

Denny sighed. "I've had that question before."

"You have? Well, that's not fair then."

"Oh, yes, it is."

"Oh, no, it isn't."

"Oh, yes, it is. Mom, just give me the pie."

Denny's mother grimaced. "All right," she said, "but you didn't win yet. You still have to make it into the center circle."

"I know that." Denny rolled the die again. A six came up.

"I don't believe it!" her mother complained. "You must be cheating."

"Mom, I'm not cheating."

"Then you're the luckiest person I ever saw. How about a rematch?"

"No, no. That's okay. I'm getting kind of tired."

"But it's only eight o'clock."

Denny shrugged.

"I know. How about if I make some hot chocolate and we turn out the lights and tell ghost stories?"

Denny thought about the *Misty Day.* "No ghost stories," she said.

"All right, just hot chocolate then."

Denny followed her mother out into the kitchen. "Ma," she said, "have you heard any of the stories about Little Hog Island?"

"Uh-huh." Her mother nodded, pouring milk into a saucepan.

"Well, how old did you hear Rufus Day was when the hurricane hit?"

"Retirement age. Sixties, I guess. Why?"

Denny shrugged. "Just wondering."

Her mother spooned some chocolate into the milk and Denny watched her stir it around.

"If you ever met a ghost," she said, "do you think you'd be able to tell?"

Denny's mother stopped stirring and looked at her. "I thought you didn't want to tell ghost stories," she said.

"I don't. I'm just wondering, that's all."

"Wondering about ghosts?"

"Yeah," said Denny. "I mean, do you think they could look like ordinary people, or do you think they have to be all . . . all . . ." She groped with her hands in the air, searching for a word. "You know," she said at last, "all floaty and see-through."

Denny's mother raised an eyebrow. "Denny," she said. "There are no such things as ghosts."

"I know that," Denny said impatiently, "but I mean, if there were."

Her mother shrugged. "I don't know," she said. "How can I give you an opinion about something that doesn't exist?"

Denny snorted. "Boy," she said, "for a writer, you sure don't have much imagination."

Denny's mother shook her head and went back to stirring. Denny sat down at the table and picked at a ragged fingernail. Her mother was right, of course, she told herself. Mr. Jones was no ghost. He was just an ordinary person.

"There's an old man living over on Little Hog Island," she suddenly said out loud.

Her mother turned and stared at her.

"A what?"

"An old man. He's living on the *Misty Day*."

Mrs. Townsend's brow furrowed. "A derelict you mean?"

Denny shook her head. "No, he's not any derelict. He's clean and well dressed, and he drives a brand-new Jeep."

Denny's mother looked at her as if she were talking nonsense. "Who told you all this?"

"Nobody told me. I saw him. I went over there today."

"You what!"

"I . . . well, I saw this smoke, and last night I thought I saw a light. . . ."

"So you just took it upon yourself to go investigate?"

Denny nodded.

Her mother threw her hands up in the air. "Well, that's just terrific. Are you crazy? Suppose he grabbed you or something? He's probably some kind of weirdo."

"He is not."

"Oh, and I suppose it's perfectly normal to be living out on an island like that at this time of year?"

"We're doing it, aren't we?" asked Denny.

"That's different."

"Why?"

"Because we're living in a house, and there's a road out here."

"Yeah? Well, plenty of people think we're loony anyway."

Denny's mother blew a fallen strand of hair out of her eyes. "So what's your point?" she asked.

"My point is that we're not loony, at least I'm not. I'm not so sure about you anymore."

Denny's mother gave her a wry smile. "So?"

"So just because Mr. Jones lives out there doesn't mean he's loony either."

Denny's mother arched an eyebrow. "Mr. Jones?"

"Well, there *are* people named Jones, you know," Denny said defensively.

Denny's mother shook her head. "It all sounds suspicious to me. I think I'm going to go into town and notify the police."

"No, Ma, don't do that."

"Denny, he could be dangerous. He could be involved in drugs or who knows what."

"He's not, Ma."

"And how do you know?"

"He has kind eyes like . . ."

"Like who?"

Denny shrugged. "Like . . . Santa Claus."

"Oh . . . oh, swell. Well, in that case . . . he's probably just over there making up a batch of toys or something."

Denny frowned at her mother's sarcasm.

"Come on, Denny," her mother said, "let's face it. At fourteen you're just not old enough to be a good judge of character."

"Yes, I am," said Denny, "especially eyes. I used to watch people's eyes on the subway all the time. Eyes tell a lot. Like yours. . . ."

Denny's mother looked at her in surprise. "Mine?"

Denny nodded and looked down at the tablecloth.

"What about mine, Denny?"

Denny's voice was quiet. "They say you're sad and scared."

There was a silence. When Denny looked up, her mother was staring at her.

"All right," she said softly. "I won't go to the police yet. But I'm going out there with you and meeting this Mr. Jones myself tomorrow."

Chapter 7

Denny pushed open the kitchen door and stuck her head inside. "Tide's almost out," she said.

"Huh?" said her mother. She was bent over her notebook, scribbling away.

"Tide's almost out. Come on."

Denny's mother looked up with that blank gaze she always got when she was writing.

Denny sighed and walked into the kitchen. She bent down and looked right into her mother's face. "Earth to Kathy," she said. "Earth to Kathy. Come in, please."

At last she saw her mother's eyes focus in on her face.

"Oh, hi," she said. "Is it time to go?"

Denny laughed and shook her head. "I worry about you, Mom," she said. "This house could burn right down around you when you're writing and you'd never notice a thing."

Her mother smiled. "I know. I'm awful. I'm sorry."

"Don't be," said Denny. "I'm glad to see you writing again." A look of understanding passed between them, and her mother nodded.

"It helps," she said. "It takes my mind off . . . things."

"Yeah," said Denny, "and maybe this book will sell and we can move back to New York."

Mrs. Townsend's smile faded. "I wouldn't count on it, Denny."

"But the last one almost did," Denny persisted, "and the publisher said maybe next time."

Denny's mother closed her notebook and sat staring at it in silence. Denny shook her head in resignation and went to get her mother's coat out of the closet.

"You'll want these too," she said, holding out a hat and a pair of mittens along with the coat.

Her mother got up from her chair and smiled. "Sometimes I wonder which of us is taking care of which," she said as she slid her arm into the coat.

"Me too," said Denny; then she grabbed her mother's hand and pulled her out the door.

Denny's mother stood on the little back stoop for a minute and breathed deeply of the salt air. Her eyes scanned the sky and came to rest on the sun-dappled sea. "Mmm," she said. "It *is* peaceful here."

"Yeah, sure," said Denny, tugging on her mother's sleeve. "Come on. The bar's got to be dry by now."

Her mother pushed her hands deep into her pockets and followed Denny down the path through the pines. "Don't you like it here, even a little?" she asked.

"No," said Denny, hurrying ahead.

"Come on. Not even a smidge?" her mother yelled.

"Why should I?" Denny yelled back.

"It's beautiful. Just look around you."

Denny reached the bar and waited for her mother to catch up. "It may have been beautiful in the summers when you were a little girl," she told her, "but now it's old, and dingy, and cold."

They started to pick their way across the bar.

"Well, I admit the cottage has run down a little since then," her mother went on, "but the island hasn't changed a bit. It was so good to see it again. Just like coming home. . . ."

Denny suddenly stopped in the middle of the bar and stared at her mother. What about my home? she felt like asking. What about the home you pulled me away from?

"What's the matter?" her mother asked.

"Nothing," said Denny. "Hey, watch out!"

An oversize wave rolled toward them, and Denny's mother shrieked and sprinted the last few feet to higher ground.

"Phew," she said, "that was close."

"This way," said Denny. She led her mother down through the blueberry bushes and scrub pines and over the cobbles to the pebbly black beach. When they neared the *Misty Day,* Denny heard a string of yips and saw Marty charging toward them. She picked up a big stick.

"Watch out," she told her mother. "That dog is part piranha. You should see what he did to my sock yesterday."

"Him?" said her mother in disbelief. "But he's so little." She bent down and put a hand out to the approaching beast, and to Denny's amazement the dog took one sniff and wiggled into her arms.

"Oh," said her mother, "he's adorable."

"Adorable?" Denny snorted.

By this time Mr. Jones had come out on the deck and was warily watching their approach. The furrow of worry came back to Mrs. Townsend's brow.

"I'm still not so sure about this," she whispered. "What kind of an oddball would want to live on an old wreck like that?"

"Probably the same kind that would want to live in an old wreck like *that*," whispered Denny, pointing back over her shoulder toward the cottage.

Her mother gave her a playful swat and then they walked the rest of the way in silence.

When they got close enough, Denny's mother shaded her eyes against the sun and looked up at Mr. Jones. "Mornin'," she said.

Mr. Jones nodded curtly. "Mornin'," he returned.

Denny's mother looked over at her, then back up. "I'm Kathy Townsend," she said. "My daughter tells me you're, uh . . . living here?"

"That's right," he said, and waited.

"Can you . . . ? I mean, is that . . . ?"

"Legal?" said Mr. Jones abruptly. "Perfectly. I own the boat and I own the island and what I do with them is my business."

Kathy Townsend's face turned red. She seemed at a loss for words. "I . . . uh, was just concerned," she said at last. "We're living over on Phinney's. . . ."

Mr. Jones's expression softened and then he stroked

his beard and chuckled. "I guess you might be at that," he said. "I guess I'd be concerned if my wife and daughter were living over there and some crazy old yahoo like me showed up."

Denny's mother smiled and relaxed.

"Come aboard," Mr. Jones offered. "I'll show you around."

Denny's mother still hesitated, but Denny was half-way up the ladder before Mrs. Townsend had a chance to protest.

The *Misty Day*, Mr. Jones told them, was a cabin sedan. She had a forecabin, which contained a kitchen and some bunks, an aft cabin, which contained more bunks, and a larger, living room kind of cabin in the middle, which served also as the wheelhouse. The boat could be steered either from the wheelhouse or from the flying bridge, which was perched up above it.

"She's a Wheeler," said Mr. Jones proudly, "a real beauty. They don't make 'em like this anymore."

Denny's mother looked around. "It needs quite a bit of work though, doesn't it?" she asked as politely as possible.

"Well, mostly cosmetics on the inside," said Mr. Jones, "fresh paint, new upholstery; the engines will have to be fully overhauled, of course. That'll be enough to keep me busy through the winter. Then I'll tackle the outside, come spring. She's got a lot of teak in her. That's why she's held up so well. She'll shape up okay."

"It's plenty warm in here," said Denny.

"Oh, yeah. She's got a wonderful old coal stove. I don't dare stoke it up full or the heat would drive me out."

"What about water and electricity?" asked Denny's mother.

"Got power already," said Mr. Jones. "I ran a cable down from the old foundation yesterday. There's water up there too, and I'm going to work on that today."

"He's an engineer," Denny told her mother.

Mr. Jones laughed. "Mostly just an old tinkerer," he said.

Denny's mother shook her head. "Seems you've thought of everything," she said.

"How do you go to the bathroom?" asked Denny.

Kathy Townsend blushed. "Denny, what a question!"

Mr. Jones laughed. "That's okay," he said. "Shows she's thinking." Then he winked at Denny and whispered, "Ghosts don't go to the bathroom."

Denny felt a tiny prickle run up her back; then she saw that her mother was laughing.

"I'm serious," she said. "How?"

"See for yourself," said Mr. Jones. He directed her into the forecabin and pointed toward a narrow door with a half-moon on it. Denny opened it. Inside, on the floor, was a little Porta Potti like the ones campers use.

When Denny came back out, Mr. Jones was still talking to her mother. "I'll need a new head, of course, before I put the boat in the water," he was saying, "but this one will do for now."

Denny stared at him and gulped. "A new head?" she repeated.

Mr. Jones laughed. "Don't look at me like you've just seen a ghost," he said. "A head is what you call a toilet on board ship."

"Oh," said Denny, laughing at herself.

"You do plan to put her in the water then?" Denny's mother asked as they climbed the steps back up to the center cabin.

"Of course," the old man said. "You don't think I want to spend the rest of my days stuck up in this cradle, do you?"

Despite her warm clothes, Denny could feel herself breaking out in goose bumps.

Mr. Jones went over and gave the *Misty Day*'s mahogany wheel an affectionate spin. "No sir," he said wistfully. "We got some sights to see yet, this old girl and me."

Chapter 8

Denny was itching to get back out to the *Misty Day*. Mr. Jones didn't look like any ghost, that was for sure, but there was something strange about the whole thing and she was determined to get to the bottom of it. Between school hours and the shifting tide schedules, though, it wasn't until the following Saturday that she was able to make the trek over the bar again.

"Be sure you don't make a pest of yourself," her mother had warned on her way to work.

"Who . . . me?" asked Denny innocently.

"And keep an eye on the tide."

"I will."

Denny heard the same high-pitched whine she'd heard the first day as she approached the *Misty Day*. Marty didn't seem to be around. She hesitated a minute at the bottom of the ladder, wondering how to announce her arrival. She tried knocking on the hull of the boat, but apparently Mr. Jones couldn't hear her over the whine. At last she decided to just go on up.

Mr. Jones wasn't on the deck, so she followed the whine through the center cabin and down into the fore. Mr. Jones was bent over an electric sander, and beyond him, Marty was curled up, sleeping on a bunk. The sander noise was deafening in the small cabin.

"Hello," Denny shouted.

Mr. Jones didn't respond.

"Hello," she shouted again.

Still no response.

Denny reached over and tapped him on the shoulder.

"Agh!" Mr. Jones shrieked, tossing the sander up in the air and clutching his chest. Marty leaped to his feet and started yapping at the top of his lungs. The sander bounced off the counter, knocking over a pile of tools, and the whole lot clattered to the floor.

Denny cringed and pressed herself against the doorway.

"Did I scare you?" she squeaked.

Mr. Jones stared at her, his chest still heaving.

"Scare me!" he said. "*Scare me!* What do you mean, sneaking up on somebody like that? You took ten years off my life, and *I* haven't got that many to spare!"

Denny shrank farther back against the steps. "I'm sorry," she said. "I tried to knock."

"*Knock!*"

"Yes, knock. You don't have a doorbell, you know."

The color was starting to come back into Mr. Jones's face and he was breathing more normally. "Well," he said gruffly, "I guess I'll have to rig one, won't I?"

Denny nodded.

Marty was still yapping away.

"Okay, okay, shush," Mr. Jones told him. Marty

36

went right on yapping. "Get a dog biscuit out of that cabinet there," Mr. Jones told Denny.

Denny found a box of Milk-Bones and took one out.

Mr. Jones was picking up his tools. Denny held the bone out to him.

"Give it to him, not me," said Mr. Jones. "Do I look like I want a Milk-Bone?"

Denny edged past Mr. Jones and held the Milk-Bone out gingerly. Marty eyed her suspiciously with one of his crooked, bulgy eyes and growled low in his throat.

"I don't think he likes me," she said.

"Apparently not," said Mr. Jones.

Denny pulled her hand back. "Well, what if he bites me?"

"Bite him back," said Mr. Jones. "You're bigger than he is."

"Yeah," said Denny, "but he's meaner."

"I'm not so sure," said Mr. Jones. "He doesn't get a kick out of scaring people half to death."

"I told you I'm sorry," said Denny. She held the biscuit out again. Either Marty was getting used to her or he was getting hungry. He stopped growling. Denny quickly placed the biscuit on the bunk in front of him and pulled her hand away. Marty snapped it up and started growling again.

"It's useless," said Denny. "He hates me."

Mr. Jones chuckled, his sense of humor apparently returning. "Dogs are supposed to be a good judge of character," he said.

Denny edged back past Mr. Jones. "All right, fine,"

she said with a huff. "I'm leaving." She climbed the steps and stomped halfway across the center cabin, then stopped. "Well," she yelled, "aren't you going to tell me not to leave?"

"No," came Mr. Jones's reply.

Denny walked back over and stared down into the cabin. "Why not?"

"Because I'm busy."

Denny put her hands on her hips. "Well, that's not very nice," she said.

Mr. Jones shook his head. "You're persistent, aren't you?" he asked.

"Well," said Denny, "there are some things I still don't understand."

"There are some things I still don't understand too," said Mr. Jones, "but I don't go bothering busy people about them."

"I *mean* about you," said Denny.

Mr. Jones sighed. "Well," he said, "I can see you're not going to leave me in peace until you get your answers, so what is it you want to know?"

"Why'd you buy this boat? I mean, for what you paid for the boat and the island you probably could've got yourself a pretty fancy new boat."

Mr. Jones snorted. "Plastic maybe," he said.

"What?" asked Denny.

"A new wooden boat like this would cost a fortune," said Mr. Jones. "Most boats today are made out of plastic."

"So?" said Denny.

"Did you ever put a piece of plastic in the water?"

asked Mr. Jones. "It sinks. Boats weren't meant to be made out of plastic."

"They're not really plastic," said Denny, "they're fiberglass."

"Same difference," said Mr. Jones.

"Well, why didn't you just buy the boat and move it to a boatyard?" Denny continued. "Why buy the whole island?"

"Because," said Mr. Jones pointedly, "boatyards tend to be full of nosy people who ask a lot of questions and waste your precious time."

Denny could feel her face flushing. "Just one more question?" she ventured.

Mr. Jones shook his head as though he was exasperated, but he said, "What?"

"Who'd you buy it from?" asked Denny.

"Man named Martin."

"Martin? What about Rufus Day?"

Mr. Jones finished sweeping up his sanding dust and went up to throw it overboard. Then he pulled open a pair of doors in the center cabin floor. Denny was right behind him.

"Aren't you gonna answer me?" she asked.

"Can't you count?" said Mr. Jones. "You had your one more question. Now, I've got work to do." He climbed down through one of the doors. Denny followed him.

"What's this?" she asked, looking around.

"Engine room," said Mr. Jones. "You'd better get on home now. You might get hurt in here."

"What are you going to do?" asked Denny.

"Got to work on these engines."

"Can't I help?"

"You know anything about engines?"

"No," said Denny. "Did you know anything about engines when you were fourteen?"

"No," said Mr. Jones. "Don't suppose I did."

"Well," said Denny, "how'd you learn?"

Mr. Jones looked at her and his mouth twisted into a grudging smile. "Okay," he said, "grab that wrench over there."

Chapter 9

Denny slept late on Sunday morning, but right after lunch she put on her hat and coat.

"You're not going over there again, are you?" asked her mother.

Denny stuck a cracker in her mouth and grunted.

"Denny, I'm not sure it's healthy for a girl like you to be spending so much time with that eccentric old man."

"He's not eccentric."

"Well, if he's not eccentric I don't know who is. Look, I saw a bunch of kids about your age skating on that little pond over on Shore Road yesterday. Why don't we take a ride over and see if they're there?"

"I don't feel like skating," said Denny. She emptied the last of yesterday's soup into a little Tupperware container.

"What's that for?"

"Mr. Jones. Ma, I saw in his cupboards yesterday. They're full of canned spaghetti and boxed macaroni and cheese and awful stuff like that."

"Denny. Mr. Jones is a grown man. He can take care of himself."

"I know that, but your homemade soup is *sooo* good, Mom. Think what a treat it will be for him."

Denny's mother smiled. "You're a con artist. You know that, don't you?"

Denny kissed her on the cheek. "I won't be long," she said.

"And stay out of that grease," her mother yelled after her.

When Denny reached the *Misty Day* she found a rope hanging over the side with a sign that said DOOR-BELL—PULL. She smiled and gave the rope a yank. There was a metallic clanging overhead and an answering string of yips came from somewhere deep inside the hull. A few seconds later Mr. Jones's bearded face peered over the side.

"You again?" he said, sounding not entirely thrilled.

Denny held up her little Tupperware container. "We had homemade soup for dinner last night," she said. "Ma thought you might like some for lunch."

Mr. Jones's icy expression melted. "You're making it very hard for me to be a hermit," he said.

"Do you really want to be?" asked Denny.

"That was the original plan."

"But my mom makes the best homemade soup," said Denny.

Mr. Jones smiled. "Okay. Come aboard."

As she came down the steps, Marty eyed her suspiciously, then broke into another string of yaps.

"All right," said Mr. Jones. "It's time you two made

friends." He picked Marty up and held him. "Come on over and pet him," he told Denny.

Denny approached warily. Marty growled low in his throat when she touched his head.

"All right, you, that's enough," Mr. Jones told him sternly.

Marty pulled his short neck in like he was sulking, but he let Denny pet him in silence. "Okay, now go on down and play," said Mr. Jones. He put Marty in a big wooden box and lowered him over the side with a kind of crane contraption.

"That's neat," said Denny. "What's it really for?"

"It's for hauling a dinghy in and out of the water," said Mr. Jones.

"Dinghy?" said Denny.

"Mr. Jones nodded. "A small rowboat," he explained.

Mr. Jones poured the soup into a little pot and set it on the coal stove to heat.

"Don't you have any friends your own age?" he asked Denny.

"Back in New York I do."

"What about here?"

Denny frowned. "They're all jerks."

Mr. Jones arched an eyebrow. "All of them?" he said.

"Yup," said Denny.

"You know what *they say* about people who think they're all right and the world's all wrong," said Mr. Jones.

"*They've* never been to this part of the world," said Denny.

Mr. Jones shook his head. "I've met a lot of nice folks around here," he said. "I don't think you're giving them a chance."

Denny folded her arms impatiently. "You sound like my mother," she said.

Mr. Jones shrugged. "Your mother seems like a sensible lady," he replied.

Denny ignored his comment and decided to change the subject. "Where'd you learn so much about boats?" she asked.

"In the navy."

"No kidding? Were you a captain or something?"

"Lieutenant," said Mr. Jones. "Commanded a repair ship."

"No wonder you know so much about fixing stuff," said Denny.

Mr. Jones laughed. "I *commanded* a repair ship," he said. "I didn't actually do the work. Most of what I do is just trial and error. I figure if someone else put it together, I can take it apart, and if I watch how it comes apart, I can put it back together again. Sometimes it works. Sometimes it doesn't."

He took his soup off the stove. "Want some?" he asked.

"No, thanks," said Denny. "I had some at home."

Mr. Jones sat down and motioned for Denny to take the seat opposite him. He dipped into the pot. "Ummm," he said. "That is good. Reminds me of the soup Martha used to make."

"Martha who?" asked Denny.

"Martha was my wife. She died about three years ago."

"Oh," said Denny. "That's too bad."

Mr. Jones nodded and didn't say anything else.

"How old was she?" asked Denny.

"Seventy-one."

Denny nodded. "Well, at least she was old."

Mr. Jones chuckled. "You tell it like it is, don't you?"

Denny shrugged. "My father died too," she said. "He was only thirty-six."

Lines of concern creased Mr. Jones's forehead. "I'm sorry to hear that," he said. "When did it happen?"

"Last summer," said Denny. "He was jogging, and he just fell down and died."

Mr. Jones stared at her compassionately. "Doesn't seem fair, does it?" he said quietly.

"No," said Denny. "It stinks."

She jumped up from the table and walked over to the sink. "These little round windows are filthy," she said.

"They're called portholes," said Mr. Jones.

"Whatever," said Denny. She picked up a paper towel and rubbed vigorously until the glass shone, on the inside at least. On the counter, next to the paper towels, she saw a picture of a young woman. "Who's this?" she asked.

Mr. Jones looked up. "That's my daughter, Andrea."

"Really?" said Denny. "Have you got any other kids?"

"No. Martha had a heart condition. We were fortunate to have had Andrea."

"Got any grandchildren?"

"No," said Mr. Jones again. There was a hint of sadness in his voice. "Andrea chose never to marry. She's a lawyer, with a very successful practice in New York."

"I don't have any grandparents either," said Denny. "Just me and my mom—that's all there is."

"That's too bad," said Mr. Jones. "I think you'd make somebody a very nice granddaughter."

Denny turned and looked at him brightly. "Really?"

"Yes, really."

She came back over and slid into the seat across from Mr. Jones again. "If I had a grandfather," she said, "I'd call him Pop."

Mr. Jones didn't say anything.

"That's a pretty good name, don't you think?" said Denny. "For a grandfather, I mean?"

"I suppose," said Mr. Jones.

Denny looked into his gentle, Santa Claus eyes. "Would you . . . if you had a granddaughter, would you like her to call you Pop?"

Mr. Jones smiled at her sadly and shook his head. "Denise," he said softly, "I don't have a granddaughter . . . and I don't want one."

Chapter 10

On Thanksgiving morning Denny lay in bed, listening to her mom bustling around in the kitchen. She didn't want to get up. Thanksgiving had always signaled the beginning of the Christmas season in their family. It was the day her father, the biggest kid of all, always got out the Christmas tapes and the Christmas books, and gave her the first gift of the season, an Advent calendar, the kind with a little chocolate candy inside each door.

Suddenly Denny heard music. It was "It's Beginning to Look a Lot Like Christmas." Then her mother was standing over her bed, holding out a gaily wrapped package.

"Happy Thanksgiving!" she said brightly.

She was smiling. How could she smile? Denny pulled the covers back over her head.

"Come on, lazybones," her mother said. "It's almost ten. Mr. Jones will be here soon."

Denny grunted.

"Don't you want to open your present?"

"Not now," Denny snapped.

There was a silence. Denny pulled back the covers

and looked up at her mother. The package hung limply from her hand and there was a look of profound disappointment on her face. "I just thought . . . ," she began.

"I can't," Denny interrupted. "Not now." She turned her face to the wall.

"Okay," said her mother softly. "I'll just leave it on the dresser." She padded quietly out of the room and Johnny Mathis abruptly stopped singing, midrefrain.

Denny sat up and swung her feet down. She flinched when they touched the ice-cold floor. She dragged her quilt into the bathroom and showered as quickly as she could. Even so, the water was only lukewarm by the time she got to rinsing her hair, and downright chilly by the time she was done. She wrapped two towels around herself, dashed back to her room, and shivered and grumbled her way into her clothes. She left the package untouched, but on her way through the living room she paused and turned the tape back on again.

Her mother smiled as she came into the kitchen. She was pulling disgusting-looking things out of the inside of the turkey.

"Feeling better?" she asked.

"I was," said Denny, turning up her nose at the bloody pile of organs. "We don't eat those, do we?"

Her mother laughed. "Some people put them in the stuffing," she said, "but I don't. I thought Mr. Jones's little dog might like them."

Denny snorted and turned away. She took a quart of milk out of the refrigerator and helped herself to a doughnut. Her mother washed her hands, poured herself a cup of coffee, and sat down.

"Is something wrong?" she asked.

Denny shook her head. "What could be wrong?"

"Well, I noticed you haven't been over to the *Misty Day* in a while, and now you don't seem too enthused that Mr. Jones is coming for Thanksgiving. Nothing *happened*, did it? I mean . . . Mr. Jones didn't . . . touch you or anything, did he?"

"No!" Denny shook her head impatiently. "Don't be stupid, Mom."

"I'm not being stupid. What am I supposed to think?"

"Nothing's wrong. I just don't see why he has to come for the whole day, that's all."

"Denny, you know he has to wait for the tides. Look, if you really don't want him to come I'll just tell him we've changed our minds—we're going out for dinner."

"No." Denny shook her head again. "I don't care if he comes. It doesn't matter anyway. Nothing matters anymore."

She got up and stomped back into her room. The wrapped present still lay on her dresser. She picked it up and hugged it to her for a moment, tears blurring her eyes; then a horrible, aching pit formed in her stomach. "It's not fair!" she shouted, hurling the package across the room. It crashed into a picture on the wall, sending it shattering to the floor, glass flying in all directions.

"Denny!"

Denny turned. Her mother stood in the doorway, her hand clasped over her open mouth. They stared at each other in silence for a few moments, until a knock came at the door. Denny's mother glanced distractedly over her shoulder, then back again. The knock persisted.

Denny finally found her voice. "That must be Mr. Jones," she said quietly. "You better let him in."

Denny's mother nodded vacantly but didn't move. The knock sounded louder.

"Go ahead," said Denny. "I'll clean this up."

Kathy Townsend turned at last and shuffled off in the direction of the kitchen. Denny got a broom and dustpan out of the front closet.

"Hello! Happy Thanksgiving," she heard Mr. Jones say.

"Flowers!" her mother exclaimed. "Where on earth did you get them?"

"Made a special trip into town yesterday," said Mr. Jones. "Wouldn't think of coming to dinner without bringing flowers for the hostess."

"Aren't you kind," said Denny's mother.

"Brought a little something else too, something to warm the insides."

Denny's mother laughed. Denny was glad to hear her laugh. She picked up the rumpled package and put it back on her dresser, then bent to sweep up the glass.

"Rrrrrr."

Denny looked up. "You?" she said. "Who invited you?"

"Rrrrrr," came the defiant reply.

Denny stared at the surly little scamp. She turned and faced him on all fours. Then she lowered her head and narrowed her eyes. "Rrrrrr," she snarled. Marty stared at her in apparent confusion. "Rrrrrr," she said again. Marty took a step backward. "Rrrrrrr," she said louder. Marty turned and skittered out of the room. Denny smiled. "You little windbag," she whispered. She swept up the rest of the glass and rehung the faded, and now glassless, print.

There was an awkward silence when Denny walked into the kitchen. It was obvious that her mother and Mr. Jones had been talking about her.

"Well, hi there," said Mr. Jones in an overly exuberant tone. "Haven't seen you in a while. How've you been?"

"Fine," said Denny. "How's the boat coming?"

"Good, good. Right on schedule." Mr. Jones sat down and pulled his pipe out of his pocket.

"Do you want a match for that?" asked Denny's mother.

"No, no. I never smoke it. I hate smoke. I just like the way it looks." He put it between his teeth and grinned.

Denny couldn't help smiling.

"Need any help there?" Mr. Jones asked Denny's mother. "I'm pretty good in the kitchen."

"Really?" Denny's mother cast a sidelong glance in her direction. "Denny seems to think you live on canned spaghetti."

Mr. Jones laughed. "Well, I eat my share, I must

admit. Seems easier most times, but I can whip up a pretty good spread when I've a mind to."

Kathy Townsend smiled. "Well," she said, "I'm all set right now, but if you're any good at gravy I'll put you to work later. That was always John's department." She hesitated when she mentioned her husband's name, and glanced at Denny. Denny turned away.

"Well, then," said Mr. Jones. "Denise, what do you say you and I go get some mussels?"

Denny eyed him skeptically. She didn't particularly want muscles. "Doing what?" she asked.

"Pardon?" said Mr. Jones.

"What do we have to do to get these muscles?" she asked.

"Cut them off of rocks."

"Cut muscles off of rocks?" said Denny.

"Yeah. They usually cling by their beards."

Denny gave him such a look of total bewilderment that her mother burst out laughing. "I think we have another communication problem here," she said. "The only muscle Denny has ever heard of is the kind in your arm."

Mr. Jones threw back his head and laughed. "Well, then, come along," he said. "It's time you learned a thing or two about the creatures you're sharing this island with."

Chapter 11

It was bitterly cold, and the newly receded tide had left a coating of ice on the beach. It was funny ice, shiny and pretty to look at, but not clear like the ice Denny was used to. It had a milky color and a grainy texture, like sherbet, only hard, and it was all bumpy and lumpy and broken up from the rocks underneath.

The sky was gray, threatening snow, and the sea was the color of steel, with wisps of sea smoke rising eerily here and there. Groups of gulls huddled together on the rocks at the water's edge as if trying to draw warmth from one another. Marty charged toward them, all fuss and fury, and they flew off in a great flurry of wings. Denny felt sorry for disturbing them.

"Do they stay all winter?" she asked Mr. Jones.

"The gulls? Yes, ma'am. They don't mind the cold."

"They look like they mind it," said Denny.

Mr. Jones chuckled. "Well, I suppose given their druthers they'd rather have a nice sunny day in June, just like the rest of us," he said, "but they take what they get and they don't complain. They're a stoic breed, a lot like the people in these parts."

Denny grimaced. "Stupid is more like it, if you ask me," she said.

"Don't recall asking you," said Mr. Jones. He walked on ahead, and Denny, feeling a bit sheepish, crossed her arms and followed him in silence.

Mr. Jones stopped beside a large group of rocks that formed a tidal pool. He put on a pair of rubber gloves, then peeled the ice away, and groped around in the water. He handed Denny a shiny black lump. "That, young lady, is a mussel."

Denny turned the lump over in her hand. "What do you do with it?" she asked.

"You eat it."

Denny made a face.

"Now, don't go turning up your nose until you've tried it. Have you ever had steamers?"

Denny nodded. "Daddy . . . my father used to love them."

Mr. Jones smiled. "Well, he would have loved these even more," he said. "They're twice as sweet and twice as tender."

He pulled a spare pair of rubber gloves from his pocket and handed them to Denny. "Just grab 'em like so," he said, "and pull. Sometimes the beards are tough, but they'll come if you yank hard."

The *beards* were the stringy filaments that anchored the mussels to the rocks. Denny soon learned the knack of grabbing close to the beard, twisting a bit, and pulling the mussel off cleanly.

"Did you ever go clamming with your dad?" asked Mr. Jones.

Denny shook her head. She didn't want to remember.

"Did he go often?" Mr. Jones persisted.

Denny shook her head again impatiently. "He never went clamming," she said. "He just ordered them in restaurants. Do we have enough of these or what?"

Mr. Jones nodded. "Yes," he said. "This should do nicely."

The little house smelled of roasting turkey when they returned, and the smell brought back another painful flood of memories.

"I'll be in my room," said Denny.

"Oh, no, you won't," said Mr. Jones. "This job's only half done. We have to clean them and cook them now."

"I don't feel like helping," said Denny. Mr. Jones and her mother exchanged glances, then her mother shook her head and shrugged.

"I owe Shell a letter," said Denny. She brushed by them both and went back to her room.

"Dear Shell," she wrote. "You're so lucky. Your life is just the way it always was."

Then there was nothing else to say. She put her head down on her bedspread and closed her eyes.

"Denny, come on, honey. Dinner's all ready. You must have dozed off."

Denny sat up and rubbed her eyes. Mr. Jones appeared behind her mother in the doorway. "Mussels are waiting," he said.

Denny got up and followed them groggily out to the

kitchen. The little table was heaped high with food, and with Mr. Jones's flowers in the middle, it was almost cheery. At each place was a steamy bowl of plump little pink mounds.

"What are those?" asked Denny.

"Those are the mussels," said Mr. Jones proudly.

"They sure look different without their shells."

"I should hope so," said Mr. Jones.

"They're delicious, Denny," said her mother. "Just wait till you try one."

Denny looked up at her mother and Mr. Jones. They were both trying so hard, she realized, to help her forget. She slid into her place at the table.

Mr. Jones and her mother sat down.

"Would you like to say grace, Mr. Jones?" her mother asked.

Denny's heart pinched. Her father had always said the Thanksgiving grace. Her mother reached out to her and they all joined hands.

"Thank you for your many blessings, Lord, for this fine food and for the company of friends"—then he looked at Denny—"and although we don't always understand your ways, Lord, may we trust in your infinite goodness."

"Amen," said Denny's mother and Mr. Jones. Denny swallowed hard. "Amen," she whispered.

"Mr. Jones brought some wine," said Denny's mother. "Would you like to try a little?"

Denny shrugged. "I guess so."

Her mother smiled. "There," she said, pouring Denny a small glass. "That will warm your tummy up."

Denny took a sip. The wine burned her throat on the way down, but spread a comforting heat in her stomach.

"Now," said Mr. Jones, "take a mussel on your fork like this, dip it in the butter broth, and pop it in your mouth."

Denny did as she was told, closing her eyes as she bit down. A sweet, buttery taste filled her mouth. "Mmm," she said, "not bad."

Mr. Jones and her mother smiled, and the atmosphere around the table relaxed. Glasses were raised and lowered, silverware clinked against china, and conversation began to flow. In time there was even laughter, and Denny was able to forget for a while.

"Oh, my lord," said Mr. Jones at last, pushing his chair back from the table and patting his enlarged stomach, "I'm about ready to burst, but I can't remember when I've had a better meal."

"Why don't you and Denny go relax in the living room," said Denny's mother, "while I clean up."

"That doesn't seem fair," said Mr. Jones. "Why don't we all pitch in?"

"There's too much clutter and the kitchen's too small," said Denny's mother. "I'll do better by myself."

"Well," said Mr. Jones, "if you insist." He and Denny walked into the living room.

"Want a fire?" he asked.

Denny shook her head. "Fireplace smokes."

"Does it now?" Mr. Jones got down on his hands and knees and peered up the flue. "Blocked," he said.

"Probably an old squirrel nest." He sat back on his heels and thought for a minute. "Be right back," he said. Before Denny could ask where he was going he had run out to his Jeep and was back with a very odd-looking contraption in his hand."

"What's that?" asked Denny.

"Toilet snake," said Mr. Jones. "You use it for cleaning clogged toilet drains, but it just might work for us here."

"Why would you keep a toilet snake in your truck?" asked Denny. "You don't even have a toilet."

Mr. Jones gave her a sheepish grin. "Tools," he said. "They're my weakness. Can't walk by a hardware store without going in and buying something, whether I need it or not. Used to drive Martha crazy." He shoved one end of the thing up the chimney and started cranking the other. There was all sorts of banging and clanking, and the next thing Denny knew a whole pile of brush and soot whooshed out of the chimney and halfway across the floor.

"What on earth?" said Denny's mother, walking into the room. Mr. Jones, covered in soot, backed out of the fireplace and looked around. He shook his head and looked up at Denny's mother. "Martha used to get so mad when I'd do things like this," he said. He looked so mortified that Denny's mother burst out laughing.

Denny couldn't help laughing too. "Your face is black," she told him. Even Marty started barking.

Mr. Jones got up and dusted himself off. "You'd think I'd learn," he said.

"Go wash up," Denny told him. "I'll get the broom."

Before long the mess was cleaned up and a merry little fire burned in the fireplace. Snow had begun to fall and the Christmas music played softly in the background. Denny couldn't help thinking how her father would have loved it all. She pretended to be reading, but the words were a blur through her tears.

"It helps to talk about it," said Mr. Jones.

Denny looked up, embarrassed that he had noticed.

"When Martha died," he said, "I kept the pain to myself for a long time, all jagged edges that tore up my insides. Then gradually I began to talk about it, and talking seemed to smooth the edges, slowly, kind of like the sea smooths those rocks out there. It still pricks now and then, of course, but mostly all I have left now are nice round memories."

Denny looked down at her book.

"This day was special for you and your dad, wasn't it?" said Mr. Jones.

Denny nodded.

"Want to tell me about it?"

"It was the beginning of Christmas," said Denny. "We'd put on the music and put up the first decoration, and we'd get out the books. . . ."

"Books?"

"We had a collection of Christmas books. My father bought me one each year ever since I was born."

Denny's mother walked quietly out of the room.

"We would read them all," Denny went on, "even the baby ones."

There was a dragging sound from Denny's mother's

bedroom, then Kathy Townsend appeared in the doorway with a cardboard box in her arms. Denny looked up. "The books," she whispered. "You brought them?"

Denny's mother lowered the box onto the table in front of her. "How could I forget them?" she said.

Denny reached into the box. The first book that she pulled out brought the tears back to her eyes, but it brought a giggle too. It was *Claude the Dog*, by Dick Gackenbach. "Daddy loved this one," she said. "It is sooo silly."

That evening as she got ready for bed, Denny remembered her mother's present. She carefully unwrapped it. Some of the chocolates had fallen out of their slots. She opened up the back and slid them back in place; then she took a thumbtack and tacked the calendar up on her door.

Chapter 12

The first nor'easter of the season blew in on Christmas Eve. The wind howled and roared outside Denny's window, driving the snow in icy sheets against the glass. The sea raged and crashed against the rocks, shaking the whole island with its booming fury. Denny got up for the third time and went to the window. She tried to stare through the swirling snow for some sign of life over on Little Hog Island. Why tonight, of all nights, to have a nor'easter?

"You're worried about him too?" Denny's mother stood in the doorway.

Denny nodded. There was another deep boom and the wind lashed at the house anew, rattling the windowpanes. "The house is shaking so," she said. "I hate to think what might be happening to the boat."

Her mother came over and put an arm around Denny's shoulders. They stared together into the fearsome night. "All I can say," she told Denny, "is that these islands have seen a lot of nor'easters over the years, and that boat must have weathered a good number of them."

Denny was unconvinced. "Maybe this is the worst one ever," she said.

Her mother smiled. "I doubt it," she said, "and besides, our standing here shivering isn't helping one bit. Let's try and get to sleep."

Denny nodded and reluctantly allowed herself to be tucked in again. Her mother sat on the edge of her bed. "I wonder how poor old Santa is faring?" she said.

Denny smiled. "Rudolph will get him through."

Denny awoke to a loud pounding. Her room was freezing and she pulled her blankets tighter. The pounding came again.

"Hey, anybody up in there?"

Denny's eyes flew open. She hopped out of bed and met her mother in the hallway.

"It's Mr. Jones!" she said.

Denny's mother was bleary-eyed. "What on earth time is it? Why is it so cold in here?"

Denny was already at the door. "Merry Christmas," shouted Mr. Jones. He burst into the room and handed Denny a package. Her mother appeared in the doorway and he handed her one too.

"Mr. Jones!" Denny shouted. "You're okay?"

"Of course I'm okay. What a beautiful day. Just wait till you step outside."

"But . . ." Denny's mother was still in a state of bewilderment. "What are you doing here so early? You weren't supposed to come over until this evening."

"Power's out," said Mr. Jones, "all up and down the coast." He started running around pulling all the shades down tight. "Help keep what's left of the heat in," he said. "Besides, I don't want you to see the

present Mother Nature left you until you step outside."

"What?" said Denny's mother.

"Just get dressed and gather up whatever you want
to bring," said Mr. Jones. "The power company esti-
mates that it'll be the better part of the day before
they get everything back on-line. You'll have to spend
the day with me on the boat where it's warm."

Denny dressed as quickly as she could, the cold
hurrying her along; then she gathered up her little
bundle of Christmas presents.

"Open the presents I brought you," Mr. Jones told
Denny and her mother. "You're going to need them."

They both pulled the paper off their gifts and found
the same present inside each: a pair of boards with
nails hammered through them and straps on top.

"Not to be ungrateful," said Denny's mother, "but
what are they?"

"You'll see," said Mr. Jones. "Just bring them along.
Have we got everything?"

"I think so," said Denny. "Gifts, food . . ."

"Okay, close your eyes."

"What?" said Denny's mother.

"Just till you get out on the porch," said Mr. Jones.
"Humor an old man, will you?"

Denny's mother laughed. "All right," she said, "but
I'd like to know what all the secrecy is about."

"You'll see in a minute," said Mr. Jones. He led
Denny and her mother out on the porch and then
announced, *"Ta-da!"*

Denny opened her eyes, and immediately her

breath caught in her throat. She stared speechless at the scene before her. Never, *ever*, in all her life had she seen anything so beautiful. Sometime during the night the snow had changed to icy rain, and now every tree, every rock, every blade of grass on the island was encased in a crystal shell. The sunlight bounced about in wild abandon, illuminating now this spun-glass sculpture, now that, as the trees swayed heavily, their branches clicking against one another in the breeze. The sky was a brilliant blue, the land pearly white, and the sea a softly rolling carpet of indigo sprinkled with sunlight sequins. Denny felt that her heart would burst from so much beauty, and she tried to draw it all in and etch it on her mind where she could keep it forever.

No one spoke for the longest time. No one wanted to. It was the closest Denny had ever felt to being in the presence of God. Denny's mother must have felt it too, because when she finally spoke she said, "I wonder if heaven could be any more beautiful than this?"

Mr. Jones smiled. "Glorious," he said. "That's the only word to describe it. A glorious Christmas morn."

Denny still said nothing. She would not go inside this day, she decided. She would stay out and just look and look and look.

"Well," said Mr. Jones, "we'd better get going before the bar covers over. You can put on your ice shoes now."

Denny and her mother looked down at the wooden

64

contraptions they held in their hands. Mr. Jones was tying a pair just like them onto his feet.

"So that's what these are?" said Denny's mother.

"Yup," said Mr. Jones. "I invented them just this morning. The crust is so thick I knew I'd never get over here and you'd never get back without them."

Denny laughed and her mother shook her head. "Mr. Jones," Mrs. Townsend said, "you never cease to amaze me."

Chapter 13

Denny lay on the couch in the center cabin, reading *The Polar Express* for at least the tenth time since Mr. Jones had given it to her that morning. "For your Christmas book collection," he had said. Denny had hugged him, and, to her surprise, he'd grown all flustered and tongue-tied, as if he had not been hugged in a very long time.

Denny gave him, in return, a wooden plaque she had found in a little gift store down the coast. It said OLD SAILORS NEVER DIE, THEY JUST GET A LITTLE DINGHY. Mr. Jones had laughed until tears ran down his cheeks. "That's me, all right," he said. "That's me." And then he'd hung it up right over the forward cabin door.

There was a small tree set up in the corner, dripping with tinsel. It had no lights, but the flickering glow of the kerosene lantern made it shimmer softly. Marty was asleep beneath it. Denny had given him a rawhide chewy bone as big as he was for Christmas, and he was worn out from wrestling with it. Mr. Jones and Denny's mother sat up in the captain's and mate's chairs by the wheel, sipping wine and talking softly.

"But why here?" Denny heard Mr. Jones ask.

Denny's mother sighed. "I'm not sure," she said. "I couldn't endure the thought of staying in New York without John. I wanted to go home, and this was the closest thing to a home that I could think of. My real home burned down when I was in college. My parents and my sister were in it."

Mr. Jones shook his head. "You've had more than your share of tragedy," he said.

Denny's mother nodded and said nothing more. She looked thin and pale and tired, and suddenly Denny's heart ached for her. Denny had been so wrapped up in her own grief lately she'd hardly given a thought to what her mother was going through. Now she went over and slid an arm comfortingly around her mother's waist. Her mother looked surprised, then grateful, and hugged her close in return.

Mr. Jones smiled at them both. He had his old captain's hat on as usual, and in the dusky light he reminded Denny once again of the Ancient Mariner.

"They think you're him, you know," she said suddenly.

Mr. Jones squinted his eyes and looked at her quizzically.

"The kids in school," Denny explained. "They think you're Rufus Day, come back from beneath the sea."

A smile played around Mr. Jones's lips. "Do they, now?" he said. "And how do they say I survived all those years?"

"They say the selkies must have found you. They say the selkies can keep a man alive for years beneath the sea, and he won't even age."

"That so?" said Mr. Jones. He nodded appreciatively and his eyes sparkled. "And what do you think?"

Denny shrugged. "I think it's a bunch of hogwash."

Mr. Jones put his smokeless pipe between his lips and leaned back and nodded.

"Well, aren't you going to deny it?" asked Denny.

"Do you want me to?"

Denny frowned. "What's that supposed to mean?"

"It means there are a lot of wonderful old tales about the sea. Who am I to say which are true and which are not?" He winked at Denny's mother.

"Stop treating me like a little kid," said Denny. "I want to know who you are, and how you knew Rufus Day, and how you came to buy this island."

"Denny," said her mother, "that's not really any of your business."

Mr. Jones shook his head. "That's all right," he said. "I don't mind telling it, if she really wants to know."

Denny nodded.

"Well," said Mr. Jones, "I first saw the *Misty Day* about five years ago. Martha and I were vacationing on the mainland and a friend took us sailing by Little Hog Island here and told us the story of Rufus Day. Mysterious old sea tales have always been something of a hobby of mine, and I was so intrigued by the *Misty Day* that I was all for inquiring into buying her right then. But Martha was a practical woman, and not being much for boats, reminded me how old I was and how much work the boat needed and basically convinced me that I was a horse's patoot. I let it drop, but I never forgot about it, and I finally decided that since Martha wasn't around to complain anymore, I could be a horse's patoot if I wanted to."

Mr. Jones leaned back again and reinserted his pipe as if the story was over.

"But what about Rufus Day?" said Denny.

"What about him?"

"How did you find him? How did you buy the island from him?"

Mr. Jones took the pipe out of his mouth and leaned forward. "I told you before," he said. "I bought this island from a man named Martin."

"But was Martin a relative or something?" Denny asked. "Didn't you ask him about the story or anything?"

Mr. Jones shook his head. "Never even met the man," he said. "Lawyers handled the whole transaction."

Denny sighed. "So that's all there is to it then?"

Mr. Jones sat back and chuckled. "Told you the old tales are more fun," he said.

It was decided that Denny and her mother would spend the night in the aft cabin since the power still wasn't back on. Mr. Jones had been using that cabin for storage so they had to move an assortment of tools and boxes off the bunks. In one of the boxes were some old photographs, and Denny couldn't help taking a peek. "Is this Martha?" she asked.

Mr. Jones looked up and smiled. "Yes," he said. He came over and took the photo fondly in his hand. "She was a beautiful woman," he said. Denny looked over his shoulder at the wrinkled little woman in the picture. Obviously Mr. Jones was seeing more than she could see when he looked into that face.

"We met on V-J Day you know."

"V-J Day?" said Denny.

"The day the Japanese surrendered, ending World War Two," he went on, apparently eager to share his memories. "My ship had just come into Virginia Beach from a tour of duty, and I was staying with some other officers in town. The whole town was jubilant and everybody was in a party mood. I saw Martha and a couple of her friends walking down the street. She was the most beautiful woman I'd ever seen." Mr. Jones looked at Denny and her mother and hesitated. "Normally I wouldn't do something like this," he said, blushing a bit. "It must have been the atmosphere that day, but I grabbed her around the waist, kissed her, and said, 'Come on, honey, we're going to a party.' She looked at me like I was crazy, but to my amazement, she went. I took her out to dinner before the party and she never ate a bite. She told me later she was scared to death."

Mr. Jones chuckled again. "I had to ship out again two days later," he said. "I was gone for a month and she wrote to me every day. When I got back I found thirty letters waiting in port. I married her that week-end."

Denny's mother smiled. "Just like in the movies," she said.

Mr. Jones nodded. "Yeah," he said, "it was." Then he raised his eyebrows. "Now mind you, I'm not claiming the marriage was always quite like the movies."

Denny's mother laughed, then her eyes grew sad. "Neither was mine," she said, "but I sure miss it, flaws and all."

Denny had pulled out an old class picture. "Is this Andrea's class?" she asked.

Mr. Jones squinted in the dusky light. "Yup," he said, "third grade. That's her right—"

"Wait," Denny interrupted. "Don't show me. Let me guess."

She looked through the rows and found two little girls who might possibly have been Andrea Jones. She looked down at the names below. "Andrea . . . *Fleming*?" she read out loud.

Mr. Jones's smile suddenly disappeared. He snatched the picture from Denny's hand. "They . . . uh . . . made a mistake that year," he said hurriedly. "They mixed Andrea up with another little girl in the third grade. Well, it's getting pretty late. We'd better hit the hay."

He got out some blankets, apologized for a shortage of pillows, took the box of photographs under his arm, and bid them both an abrupt good-night.

Denny lay in the darkness on the lumpy old bunk. It felt damp and smelled of salt and mildew.

"Ma?" she whispered.

"Yeah?"

"Why do you think Mr. Jones doesn't want us to know who he really is?"

"I don't know, Denny, but whatever his reasons, I think we ought to respect them."

Chapter 14

The winter passed slowly on the island, but it wasn't a bad slow, it was a good slow, a healing slow. Denny took long walks by herself and came to know the sea in all its many moods and the island in its myriad garbs, from autumn green, to winter white, to misty, shrouded gray. Ice seemed ever present on the island. It cascaded from the cliffs below the lighthouse in hues that ranged from palest blue to deep, mustardy yellow. It built up heavily on the shorefront trees, layer upon layer, until Denny wondered at the inner strength that kept them from toppling into the sea. It formed great cakes on the beach, which piled one on the other, some floating back out on the tides, but others remaining for Denny to climb on and explore.

Denny came to know the island creatures too, the deer, the rabbits, the winter birds . . . came to know them in a way that the old Denny, the busy, hurried, noisy Denny, never could. Once, to her delight, she even surprised a harbor seal, basking on the rocks on the front of the island. It had looked at her for a long time with its gentle, puppyish face before sliding silently back into the sea.

Winter seemed to be a healing time for Denny's mother too. Denny no longer heard sobs in the night, and more and more her mother threw herself into her new book, a love story, Denny discovered, about a woman named Kathy and a man named John.

Denny made such a pest of herself over at the *Misty Day* that Mr. Jones finally decided that the only way to get on with his work was to put her to work right beside him. He even went so far as to give her her own engine to work on. "I'll take the port engine," he told her, "and you take the starboard. Watch me and do everything I do, and heaven help you if my engine starts come spring, and yours doesn't."

"And heaven help you if *my* engine starts come spring and *yours* doesn't," Denny answered.

She named her engine Stella because it started with an *S*, like starboard, and she named Mr. Jones's engine Penelope because it started with a *P*, like port. Before long she was boring her mother to tears at dinner, babbling about manifolds, carburetors, gaskets, and fuel pumps.

When Denny and Mr. Jones weren't working on engines, they were painting, varnishing, and replacing sections of the boat that had dry rot. As long as Denny didn't ask too many questions, things went smoothly, except when Mr. Jones made mistakes, and he made a lot of them. Sometimes he'd get so mad he'd get tears in his eyes.

"How can I be so stupid?" he'd mumble. "I measure everything twice, and still I make mistakes."

"I don't know why you get so mad at yourself," Denny'd told him. "I make mistakes all the time."

"Yes," Mr. Jones had said tiredly, "but you're young. You know you'll get better. I've been better, and I'm afraid I'll only get worse."

Now Denny tried hard to be his extra eyes and tactfully catch mistakes before they happened.

Another thing that worried her was that Mr. Jones had begun to limp. She'd mentioned it once, and he had snapped at her and told her he'd never felt better, so she'd never mentioned it again, but she worried just the same.

Spring seemed to come on at a snail's pace, bringing to the islands little more than a slight gentling of the ever-present wind, but nevertheless, by late March more and more boats were moving in and out of the harbor, and the shore seemed to be coming back to life. Mr. Jones went out and bought a little dinghy, which gave them both a good laugh, but it made getting back and forth across the sandbar a lot simpler. Mr. Jones gave Denny his portable air horn, and whenever she wanted a ride across, she'd just give it a toot and he'd come get her.

One morning, when the bar was passable and Denny had walked across, she was surprised to spy a shabby red speedboat pulled up on the beach beside the *Misty Day*. Did Mr. Jones buy that too? she wondered. But as she approached she heard voices coming from the old shack that housed the engine for the marine railway.

When two figures emerged, Denny winced. What on earth was Mr. Jones doing with *that* loser? Marty was trotting happily alongside the pair. "Some judge of character *he* is," Denny mumbled to herself.

Mr. Jones waved. "Denny," he said. "Come here. I want you to meet my new hired hand."

Denny's mouth fell open and she stood motionless as the two approached. Spence grinned at her in his aggravating, superior way.

"Well, if it isn't Miss High and Mighty from *New Yawk.*"

"You know each other?" said Mr. Jones.

"We've met," said Denny shortly, then she turned and stomped off toward the boat. She watched from the cabin as the two circled the *Misty Day*, talking and gesturing; then Spence went back toward the engine shack and Mr. Jones made his way slowly up the ladder.

"Are you crazy?" Denny asked him as soon as he stepped into the cabin.

Mr. Jones smiled. "Some people seem to think so," he said.

"I mean it," said Denny, in no mood for jokes. "That kid is the biggest jerk in the whole school. He's probably into drugs and everything else."

Mr. Jones shrugged. "Seems like an okay kid to me," he said. "Besides, he knows engines."

"So do you," said Denny. "We could have fixed the railway ourselves."

"We're running out of time," said Mr. Jones.

"Time for what?" said Denny. "You're retired. You have all the time in the world."

Mr. Jones looked at her, and there was a momentary flicker of sorrow in his eyes. "The *Misty Day* has to be in the water by the end of June," he said quietly.

"But why?"

"Because . . . because that's when the boating season starts, and I want to take full advantage of it."

"To do what?"

"To go to sea."

Denny turned away abruptly. Mr. Jones had not mentioned going to sea since that first day, back in November, and somehow Denny had hoped he'd changed his mind, or at least that he wouldn't be going for a long time. The news that he meant to go so soon came as a shock to her.

"How long will you be gone?" she asked.

Mr. Jones didn't answer. When she turned back, she thought the sorrow was there again, but he brushed it off quickly. "Now, how can I think that far ahead?" he said brusquely. "Got enough to worry about between now and June." He hobbled off toward the aft cabin. Denny saw him wince as he started down the steps. She followed after him.

"There's something wrong with your leg," she said. "I think it's time you saw a doctor."

"I think it's time you minded your business," said Mr. Jones. He bent down and picked up his heavy tool chest.

Denny sniffed. "Now where are you going?" she

asked as he brushed by her and started back up the stairs.

Mr. Jones ignored her question. "Pigheaded old fool," she mumbled to herself. She climbed the stairs and stomped past him.

"Where you goin'?" he asked.

"Home," she said shortly.

"In that case, would you take this wrench set on up to Spence at the shack?"

Denny stared at him, tempted to tell him to take it himself, but then her concern over his leg got the better of her. "Yeah, sure," she grumbled, grabbing the wrenches from his hand.

Marty was lying in the sun outside the shed when she got there. He opened one eye and looked up at her suspiciously. "Grrrr," he said.

"Oh, grrrr yourself," she snapped at him.

Spence stuck his head out the door. "Well, looky who's here," he said, "her Royal Highness. Come to pay a call?"

Denny scowled at him. "Mr. Jones said to give you these," she said, holding out the wrenches.

He reached for them; then, as she started to turn away, he grabbed her hand. "Wait a minute," he said.

Denny pulled her hand away.

"What do you want?"

Spence held his two hands up as if she had a gun pointed at him. "Take it easy," he said. "I'm just trying to be friendly."

"I don't need your kind of friends," Denny spat.

Spence narrowed his eyes. "Oh, yeah?" he said. "Well, it don't seem to me like you been winning any popularity contests lately."

"Maybe I don't care," said Denny; then she whirled and stormed away.

Chapter 15

With the weather turning milder and most of the inside work done, Denny and Mr. Jones had begun working on the outside of the boat. Mr. Jones had just started her on scraping the bottom when he came around the bow and stopped short. He shook his head in disbelief.

"How did you manage to get so filthy so fast?" he said. "Didn't I tell you to wear a painter's cap?"

Denny shrugged and squinted at him through her safety goggles. "I thought the wind would blow the old paint and junk away as I scraped it off," she said.

Mr. Jones came over and took a closer look. "Look at your hair," he said. "Your mother's going to kill me. Try and shake some of that junk out of it."

Denny leaned over and shook her hair in the wind. She was almost sorry she'd let it grow. Long hair was such a pain sometimes. She heard the putter of an outboard motor and looked up to see Spence making his way across the bay.

"Him again," she grumbled, but she pulled the comb out of her back pocket and started furiously tugging at her hair.

Mr. Jones grinned. "Thought you couldn't stand him," he said.

"I can't," said Denny, whipping off her safety glasses.

"Oh," said Mr. Jones; then he gave her a maddening smile and went back to rebuilding the cradle.

Denny glanced at Spence out of the corner of her eye as he approached. He stood at the wheel, wearing a knit sailor's cap and an old navy peacoat. A shock of blond hair stuck out under the cap and was swept back by the wind. His dark eyes squinted into the sun, and the cut of his jaw was firm and square. Denny shook her head. "You've been away from civilization too long," she told herself, "when somebody like him starts looking good."

Spence beached the boat and strutted up to where Denny and Mr. Jones were working. He stared at Denny and smiled. "You got enough of that shit on your face?" he asked.

Mr. Jones looked up sharply. "What's the matter with you?" he said. "You don't talk to a lady like that."

Spence laughed. "What lady?" he said.

Denny blushed. She could see the anger building in Mr. Jones's eyes. "It's all right," she said quickly. "I don't care."

Mr. Jones turned to her. "Well, you should," he told her, his eyes flashing, "and Mr. Spencer here would respect you more if you did, whether he realizes it or not."

Spence snorted derisively.

"Well, like it or not, you keep a civil tongue while you're working for me, mister, understand?" said Mr. Jones.

Spence shrugged. "You're the boss," he said, and started walking up toward the shack.

Mr. Jones picked up a nail. "You kids today use too darn much profanity anyway," he yelled. He banged the nail into the brace. "You use it anytime, anyplace. It's not right." He banged another nail. "Shows a lack of respect, not to mention a deficient vocabulary." He slammed another nail into the wood. "There's a time and a place for profanity." He held another nail and smashed the hammer down. "Aagh! Like now! Dammit!" He dropped the hammer and grabbed his thumb.

Denny covered her mouth and turned away so he wouldn't see her laugh, but he saw anyway.

"Oh, very funny, huh?" said Mr. Jones.

Denny couldn't stop giggling. Soon she had Mr. Jones laughing too. "That's what I get for trying to defend your honor," he said.

"Sorry," said Denny. She looked up the hill and saw Spence duck into the shed. There was a burst of loud, muffled laughter, and she started giggling all over again.

"All right, all right," said Mr. Jones. "Are you going to go get me a Band-Aid or do I have to stand here and bleed to death while you and your friend up there make sport of me?"

Denny took a deep breath. "He's not *my* friend," she reminded him. "Where do you keep the Band-Aids?"

"In the cabinet in the head."

"Where else?" said Denny.

She climbed the ladder and hurried down to the little bathroom. There was a small cabinet on the wall and she found the Band-Aids and a tube of first-aid cream. She turned to leave, but something caught her eye. It was an old, leather-bound book, tucked into a rack on the wall along with a bunch of magazines. It wasn't the age of the book that made her stop, though, it was the name on the front—*Rufus Day*! Denny gently lifted the book from the rack, her heart thumping in her chest. SHIP'S LOG, it said. CAPTAIN, RUFUS DAY. Denny's hand trembled as she opened it up. The pages were yellowed and brittle.

"October 12, 1954," was the first entry. "Having escaped the devastation of my home by fleeing aboard ship full in the face of a hurricane, and having successfully ridden out that hurricane at sea, I take it as an omen that I am meant to spend my remaining days at sea, and I now set forth, keeping here a journal of my days. . . ."

There was a sudden sound and Denny looked up to see Mr. Jones looking down at her, his eyes filled with silent fury.

"I . . . uh . . . I saw it in the rack," she stammered.

Mr. Jones said nothing. He took the book from her hand, closed it quietly, and turned away.

"You . . . you said you never knew Rufus Day," Denny stammered.

Mr. Jones kept his back to her. "I don't think I owe you any explanations," he said, his voice taut.

Anger rose inside her. "I've been helping you all winter," she said, "working right beside you. If it wasn't for me, you'd never have this boat ready by June. The least you could do is tell me what's going on."

Mr. Jones turned to look at her, his face like stone. "Helping was your idea," he said, "but you're right. I do owe you something. If you'll figure it out, I'll gladly pay you for your time."

"Pay me?" Tears of anger sprang to Denny's eyes. "I thought I was your friend." She threw the Band-Aids down on the nearest bunk. "There," she said, starting up the ladder, "call your hired hand and get him to help you with your thumb."

Chapter 16

Denny shoved her books into her locker and pulled out her coat.

"Going to work for old Rufus this afternoon?" she heard someone say. There was a burst of laughter, and Denny turned. The question wasn't directed at her though, she discovered, but at Spence, who was just coming down the stairs. Denny busied herself in her locker, hoping no one would notice her.

"He's no more Rufus Day than I am," she heard Spence say. "He's just some crazy old blow-in with a fat bankroll and a lot of time on his hands." Spence's gang laughed. "Leave it to Spence to help relieve an old outsider of his bankroll," someone said. "Need any help, Spence?"

"Nah," said Spence, "I think I can manage."

Denny narrowed her eyes and glared at Spence's back as he went by. So that's what he was up to. Well, it wasn't any business of hers. The way she figured it, Mr. Jones deserved whatever he got.

The Jeep was parked at the beginning of the causeway when Denny got off the bus. She ignored it and started toward the island.

"Denise . . ."

Denny ignored Mr. Jones's call and kept on walking.

She heard the engine start, and soon the Jeep was rolling along beside her.

"Picked up your mail," said Mr. Jones. He handed some envelopes out the window. Denny grabbed them without a word.

"There's a letter there from some old coot named Jones," Mr. Jones said. "Looks like an apology."

Denny looked down and ruffled through the envelopes. "There is not," she said.

"No?" said Mr. Jones sheepishly. "Well, there should be. Guess he didn't get around to writing it. He feels real bad though. I know that for a fact."

Denny stopped and put her hand on her hip and stared at Mr. Jones. The Jeep stopped rolling.

"How about a ride?" he said. "We'll talk about it."

Denny let out an exaggerated sigh, but she walked around the Jeep and climbed in on the passenger side. Mr. Jones took his foot off the brake.

"Us dinghy old sailors," he began, "we get pretty cranky sometimes, and for no real good reason."

Denny rolled her eyes at him. "What about the book?" she said.

"What about it?"

"Why were you hiding it?"

"I wasn't hiding it. What makes you think I was hiding it? It was right in the head. Why don't you accuse me of hiding magazines? They were in the same rack."

Denny snorted. "You don't get mad when I read your magazines," she said.

"I told you I'm sorry. I was just aggravated because you were taking so long with the Band-Aids."

Denny narrowed her eyes. "Then where did you get the book? You said you never knew Rufus Day."

"It was in the boat," said Mr. Jones, "in one of the cupboards under the bunks. I just found it the other day."

"Oh, really?" said Denny, not quite ready to believe him. "Then why didn't you tell me?"

"Didn't have a chance," said Mr. Jones. "Besides, there's not much to tell. It must've gotten wet at some point. Only the first page is legible."

Denny eyed him skeptically. "Can I see it, then?" she asked.

Mr. Jones reached over the back of the seat and grabbed something. "Suit yourself," he said, dropping the book in her lap.

Denny opened it eagerly. It looked different. It seemed much thicker, and the pages were more wrinkled than she remembered, like . . . like someone had wet them and then dried them out again. She turned the first page. He was right. Everything else was just a blur. Denny stared down at the book. Should she challenge him again and risk losing his friendship, or should she, as her mother had said, respect his wish to keep up his charade?

"That's too bad," she said at last. "I guess now we'll never know what happened to Rufus Day."

Mr. Jones shrugged. "Evidently he survived the hurricane and went to sea," he said. "My guess is he just got old and feeble and probably fell overboard."

Denny nodded. "Probably," she agreed.

"Well," said Mr. Jones, obviously pleased to have that portion of the conversation behind them, "the parts came in. Shall we give old Stella and Penelope a new lease on life?"

Denny shrugged. "Sure," she said. "Why not?"

When they neared the sandbar Denny could see Spence's boat already making its way across the bay.

"I don't know if I should tell you this or not," she said, "but I overheard Spence and some of his friends talking in school today. He said something about relieving you of your bankroll."

Mr. Jones's brow furrowed. "Spence said that?" he asked.

Denny nodded.

Mr. Jones sighed and shook his head. "Well, thanks for telling me," he said. "I'll keep my eyes open."

"You mean you're going to let him keep working for you?" said Denny incredulously.

Mr. Jones nodded. "I don't like the sound of what you heard either," he said, "but I'm usually a pretty good judge of character, and I think Spence is okay. A little rough around the edges maybe, but basically okay."

"How can you say that?" Denny asked.

"His eyes," said Mr. Jones. "You can tell a lot by people's eyes. Have you ever really looked in Spence's eyes?"

Denny stared at him. "No," she said quietly. "I guess not."

Chapter 17

They had to park the Jeep, load the engine parts into the dinghy, and row across the bar, so by the time they reached the *Misty Day* Spence was already there, leaning against the cradle, puffing on a cigarette.

Mr. Jones frowned when he saw him. "How old are you?" he asked.

"Sixteen," said Spence. "Why?"

"Do you know what your lungs are going to look like by the time you're fifty?"

Spence shrugged, then nodded toward the ever-present pipe that hung from Mr. Jones's lip. "No worse than yours, I guess," he said.

Mr. Jones looked puzzled.

"He means your pipe," Denny prompted.

"Yeah," said Spence, "and don't give me any of that crap about a pipe being not as bad as a cigarette. They're all the same."

Mr. Jones took his pipe out of his mouth and looked at it thoughtfully.

"You know," he said, "you've got a point there. Kind of like the pot calling the kettle black, isn't it?"

Spence nodded.

"Tell you what I'm going to do," said Mr. Jones. "I'll make you a little wager. I'll bet I can give up smoking my pipe if you can give up your cigarettes."

Denny bit her lip to keep from smiling.

Spence took another drag on his cigarette and stared at Mr. Jones skeptically.

"Of course, if you don't think you've got the will-power," said Mr. Jones.

Spence dropped his cigarette and crushed it into the ground. "I can quit anytime I want," he said, then looked up. "But I don't want to."

"Oh, sure," said Denny. "That's what they all say."

Spence looked at her and narrowed his eyes. "Who asked you?" he said.

"You just don't think you can do it," Denny went on. "You're afraid Mr. Jones is gonna show you up."

"Oh, yeah?" said Spence. He pulled his cigarettes out of his jacket pocket, smiled wryly at Denny, and tossed them basketball style into Mr. Jones's trash barrel, then reached a hand out to Mr. Jones. "You got a deal, old man," he said.

Mr. Jones shook his hand and nodded, then stuck the pipe back in his mouth. "You don't mind if I just kind of let it hang here, do you, for old times' sake?"

Spence shrugged. "Suit yourself," he said, "long as you don't light up."

"I'm a man of my word," said Mr. Jones. "No flame will ever touch this pipe again."

Spence nodded and stalked off toward the shed.

Denny giggled. "You're awful," she said.

Mr. Jones winked. "What's awful?" he said. "I'm doing him a favor."

Denny and Mr. Jones loaded the engine parts into Marty's box, then went up into the boat and hauled them up. Marty was yipping to go down, so Mr. Jones lowered him over the side. Denny watched him jump out of the box and run as fast as his stubby legs would carry him up to Spence at the shed. Denny shook her head. There was just no figuring that dog out.

"Darn it anyway," said Mr. Jones. He had the parts all spread out on the floor.

"What's the matter?" asked Denny.

"Oh, nothing," said Mr. Jones. "It's just that this belt is for the railway engine. I meant to give it to Spence." He started to get laboriously to his feet.

"I'll take it up," said Denny. "You stay right there."

Mr. Jones started to protest, but Denny grabbed the belt and started down the ladder before he had the chance.

Marty growled as usual when she walked by and she resisted the urge to give him a kick. She found Spence tinkering with the engine, so deep in thought he didn't seem to know she was there.

"Uh-hum," she said.

"Yeah," said Spence, without looking up.

"Mr. Jones said this belt is for you."

"Oh, good," said Spence, "I've been waiting for that."

Denny handed him the belt and went back out. She was almost back to the boat when there was a loud metallic snap and suddenly the *Misty Day* and her cradle lurched and began to move slowly down the rails toward the water. Denny screamed.

Spence came barreling out of the shed. "Oh, my *God!*" he shouted.

"What's happening? What's wrong?" Denny shrieked.

Spence ran by her. "I had to undo the chain," he yelled. "I thought the brake would hold, but it must have been rusted through."

Mr. Jones came up on deck. His face was white. "What on earth is going on?" he shouted.

"I had to undo the chain," Spence repeated. "I thought the brake would hold."

Mr. Jones grabbed his head and shook it. The *Misty Day* was picking up speed. "You've got to get the engine going," he yelled. "Her seams are wide open. She'll go down like a lead sinker."

Spence scrambled back up the hill and Denny followed, her heart pounding. Spence ducked into the shed. Denny was right behind him.

"What can I do?" she asked.

"Stay out of the way," Spence growled. He stood staring helplessly as the winch rolled freely, playing out more and more chain.

Denny stared at him angrily. "Well, do something!" she yelled.

"I can't!" he yelled back. "Do you know how much force is turning that thing?"

Denny ducked back outside. "The cradle's almost in the water!" she screamed. "We've got to stop it."

She looked around desperately. There was a pile of old timbers a short distance away. She ran over and grabbed a couple and dragged them back. "Spence, help me!"

Spence poked his head out the door and seemed immediately to grasp what she had in mind. Without a word he grabbed one of the timbers and dragged it inside. Between the two of them they managed to wedge it between the wall and the winch. The drum came to a stop. The chain groaned, stretched, and held.

"Get the other one," Spence yelled. Denny ran out for the other timber. The *Misty Day* was belly deep in water.

"Hurry," shouted Mr. Jones. "The waves are going to knock the cradle to pieces."

Denny dragged the timber in and wedged it behind the first while Spence went to work connecting the new drive belt.

"Okay," he said, "now pray that the engine starts."

He flipped the switch and the engine turned dryly a couple of times, then sputtered, coughed, and caught.

"Yeah!" shouted Denny.

"All right," said Spence. "When I give you the word, shove those timbers out of the way. Okay . . . *now!*"

Denny shoved. The timbers fell and the chain began slowly rewinding.

Denny poked her head out of the door. The *Misty Day* was moving steadily back up the rails. "It's working!" she shouted.

"Of course it's working," Spence bragged. "You're talking to a master mechanic."

Denny nervously eyed the waves that were buffeting the boat. "Can't it go any faster?" she asked.

"Sure," said Spence.

He stepped back inside the shed. The roar of the engine grew louder and the *Misty Day* lurched and began to move more rapidly. She was almost to the shore when she came to an abrupt stop again and the motor died.

"Now what?" yelled Denny. She poked her head back into the shed.

"I don't know," said Spence, shaking his head in confusion. "She was running fine. . . ."

"What about the chain?" asked Denny.

"The chain should hold right where it is for now."

Denny ran down to the shore. The *Misty Day* was just a few feet out of the water.

"Something happened to the engine," she shouted. "Will you be okay for a while?"

Mr. Jones looked around. "For a little while," he said. "But those waves are going to play havoc again the more the tide comes in."

"We'll fix it before then," said Denny. "Don't worry."

Mr. Jones didn't look convinced. "If it wasn't for this dumb leg," he shouted, "I'd jump ship and give you a hand."

"No need," yelled Denny, "I remember everything you taught me."

Mr. Jones shook his head and smiled. "That's what I'm afraid of," he said.

Denny hurried back up to the shed. Spence was

staring at the engine with a look of profound befuddlement.

"What's the problem?" asked Denny.

Spence shook his head. "Nothing you'd know anything about."

Denny bristled. "Try me," she said.

Spence stared at her, and a bemused smile crossed his lips. "Okay," he said. "The problem is, it was running, and now it's not."

Denny gave him a scornful smirk. "You're a big help," she said. "Move over."

Spence stepped aside with an exaggerated bow.

Denny examined the engine. "Odds are it's electrical," she said. "Ninety percent of all engine problems are electrical."

Spence raised an eyebrow and looked at her.

"Battery looks new," she went on.

Spence nodded.

"How about the plugs?"

"New too," said Spence.

"The coil?"

Spence's mouth was starting to hang open. "Old, but okay," he said.

"And the rotor?"

Spence shook his head. "How do you know so much about engines?" he asked.

Denny smiled. "I've had a good teacher," she said.

"Mr. Jones?"

Denny nodded.

Spence shrugged. "Rotor's turning fine," he said.

"How about the starter then?"

95

"I cleaned it all up. It's fine too."

"Then it's got to be the distributor," said Denny.

Spence shrugged again. "I cleaned it and replaced all the wires," he said. "It should be okay."

"Look," said Denny, "it's the only thing left. Let's take it apart and check it again."

Spence grudgingly dismantled the distributor.

"Damn!" he said. Then he looked at Denny. "Oh, pardon me," he said. "I mean, darn!"

Denny grimaced. "Just tell me what's wrong," she said.

"It's the spring on the points," he said. "Must have been too much for it when I gunned the engine."

"Well, fix it," said Denny.

It was Spence's turn to smirk. "I can't fix it," he said. "We need a new set of points."

Denny shook her head firmly. "We've got to fix it," she said. "We have no time to wait. Mr. Jones says where there's a will there's a way. Now tell me how it works."

Spence shook his head like it was hopeless, but he explained the mechanics of the distributor to Denny.

"So the spring only holds the moving part of the points to the rotor?" Denny asked.

"That's right, but without it, no spark."

Denny pulled a rubber band out of her hair. "We can do the same thing with this," she said.

Spence scowled. "Are you crazy?" he said. "That'll never last."

"We don't need it to last," said Denny. "We just need it to work now."

96

"Nah, it'll never work," said Spence.

Denny narrowed her eyes. "Have you got a better idea?" she asked.

Spence didn't answer.

"Then do it," said Denny.

Spence took the rubber band and halfheartedly rigged it to the distributor. Then he reconnected the distributor to the engine.

"Ready?" he said.

Denny crossed her fingers. "Ready," she answered.

Spence flipped the switch and the engine started with such a roar that they both clapped their hands over their ears and ran out of the shed. Denny collapsed, laughing, against the shed wall.

"I guess it works," she shouted.

"Guess so," yelled Spence, giving her a reluctant grin. Mr. Jones hollered over from the deck and gave them the thumbs-up sign as the *Misty Day* resumed her gradual climb to safety. Spence saluted in return.

Denny straightened up. "That was close," she said, noting how far the tide had advanced.

Spence stuck his hands into his back pockets and nodded.

Denny turned to go.

"Hey," said Spence.

Denny turned back. "Yeah?"

Spence grinned. "Thanks."

Denny looked into his eyes and felt her cheeks growing warm. She nodded, then turned and raced down the hill.

Chapter 18

Denny saw him get on the bus the next afternoon and she could feel him moving down the aisle. She stared at her books, willing her traitorous heart to stop flopping around in her chest. I don't like him, she told her heart. He's nothing like the boys in New York. He's crude and stupid, and a loser.

"Mind if I sit down?"

Denny could feel herself turning red, like a thermometer in the sun, the hot flush creeping up her neck to her cheeks. She shook her head and Spence slid into the seat beside her. He balanced his books on his knee. Denny couldn't help noticing the book on the top. It was *The Red Badge of Courage*.

"You reading that for English?" she asked.

Spence shook his head. "No," he said, "I'm just reading it."

"For fun?" said Denny.

Spence nodded.

"But that's a hard book."

The warmth went out of Spence's eyes and his brows knit together. "I *can* read, you know," he said harshly. "I even get good grades, and I plan to go to college.

A lot of us country bumpkins do. Does that spoil your image? Make you feel less superior?"

Spence jumped to his feet just as the bus lurched into motion. He clutched his books and staggered down the aisle.

"Hey, you! Sit down!" yelled the bus driver.

"Yeah, yeah," Spence muttered.

Denny clenched her teeth together and stared out the window. The vacant seat beside her seemed to echo the emptiness she felt inside. Maybe they were right; her mother, Mr. Jones, Spence. . . . She turned and looked over her shoulder. Spence was crammed into a seat that already had two people in it, his long legs sticking out into the aisle. He knew she was looking at him, she could tell, but he stared straight ahead, his face like stone. She pulled a sheet of paper out of her binder and scribbled a note. She leaned over the seat.

"Would you pass this to Spence?" she asked the girl behind her. She saw Spence's eyes flicker momentarily in her direction and back, but his jaw remained set. The girl looked annoyed, but she took the note and turned and shoved it under Spence's nose. Spence grabbed it, but he made no attempt to read it, and Denny turned at last with a sigh and spent the rest of the ride staring out the window and calling herself names under her breath.

When Denny stepped from the bus, she was surprised to hear another set of footsteps land behind hers. She turned to find Spence standing there, the open note in his hand. The bus roared away and they were all alone, with nothing between them but the wind. Denny took a deep breath and tried to smile, but her lips felt trembly. Then suddenly she was crying.

Spence looked surprised and concerned. "What's wrong?" he asked.

Denny shook her head. "I don't know. I've been such a jerk."

Spence's eyes softened. He reached up and brushed the tears from her cheeks. "Hey, that's okay," he said. "You've had a rough year, your dad dying and all."

Denny looked at him. "How did you know?" she asked.

Spence smiled. "Word gets out around here," he said. "Come on. I'll walk you home."

"But that's out of your way," Denny said.

Spence shrugged. "I'm going out to the *Misty Day* anyway. I'll get Mr. Jones to drive me home later."

As they walked, Spence reached out and took her hand. His touch sent a warmth surging through her, and for a few minutes Denny couldn't speak at all.

"Cormorants are back," said Spence, gesturing with his books toward a flock of homely, buzzardlike birds that were clustered on the rocks offshore.

Denny nodded. The warmth was turning into a happy glow.

"The island seems to agree with you," said Spence.

Denny found her voice. "What do you mean?" she asked.

"You look real pretty," said Spence, "with your cheeks all pink and your hair long like that."

Denny blushed. She'd realized, of course, that she looked different with her hair long, but she'd never dreamed that a boy like Spence might find her pretty. For the second time since she'd come to the island, Denny felt like she could fly.

Chapter 19

Denny's mother burst into the kitchen, her eyes all aglow.

"Denny, you won't believe it. The publisher called. He's interested in the book. He wants me to fly to New York to talk about a possible contract!"

Denny jumped up from the couch and ran out to give her mother a hug. "That's great, Mom," she shouted. "When?"

"He said within a week or two. He's going to call me back. Oh, Denny, I'm afraid to let myself hope too much, but I can't help it."

Denny smiled. "They'll take it. I know they will. You're a good writer, Mom."

Denny's mother squeezed her tight. "Oh, I hope so. I hope so. I wish I could take you with me, if only we could afford another plane ticket."

"That's all right. I'll be fine."

"I'll only be gone a day. I'll catch an early morning flight and be back the same night."

"Don't worry about it, Mom. I'll be okay."

Denny's mother sat down on a chair and pulled her close. "Denny, if this happens . . . if they buy the book . . . we can go back to New York."

Denny's heart skipped a beat. "Really?"

"Yes. Maybe I shouldn't have said anything yet. I don't want to get your hopes up. But we'd have enough money, and I think I can face going back now."

"*All right!*" said Denny. "I gotta write and tell Shell!"

"I said *if*, remember," her mother called after her as she raced into the bedroom.

Denny grabbed her writing paper and flopped down on the bed. It was late May and the windows were open. It was still cool, much cooler than New York in May, but the air felt soft after the harshness of winter. *Keer-keer*, she heard, the cry of a tern. Spence had told her all about them, how they wintered in Antarctica and returned all those thousands of miles each spring to the exact place of their birth. Spence called them a marvel. It seemed a funny word for him to use, but she was discovering much about Spence that surprised her.

Suddenly Denny didn't want to write to Shell at all. She pulled a sweatshirt over her head and went out for a walk. The island was turning a soft green, gentle to the eyes after the sharp contrasts of winter. There was a fresh, earthy smell to the air. Here and there violets peeked out from among the pine needles, and the shadbush trees, which had been hidden among the pines all winter, now gloriously announced their presence with profusions of soft pink blossoms.

Denny went out on the bluff and sat down, her chin resting on the lower part of the railing. The sea washed hypnotically in and out, in and out. How many nights had she fallen asleep to that soothing rhythm? An osprey sailed into view, hovering momentarily overhead, its great white wings majestic against the clear blue sky. Then without warning it plunged, feet first into the sea, rising up again with a fish wriggling in its talons. Denny watched it veer off toward the mainland, presumably to a nest where hungry chicks waited.

Denny took a deep breath, her heart strangely full. It would be good to get back to New York, she tried to tell herself. There would be shows, movies, parties, shopping, kids that spoke her language. . . .

She got up and put her hands into her pockets and ambled down to the bar. It was low tide and she walked across, then followed the path her own footsteps had worn down to the shore. The *Misty Day* was perched at the water's edge now. Mr. Jones had moved her down so the incoming tides would lap at her bottom and help her newly compounded seams to swell. It would take a week or so, he said, then he would launch her and let her swell a few more days before he hooked the drive shafts up to the engines. Denny looked at the boat with pride. No one would believe, looking at her now, that she had been an old wreck just seven months ago. She glistened with new paint and varnish, and her brass was polished till it shone. Spence, who had surprised them with an artistic bent, had refurbished her name. She wore it proudly now in shining red and gold—MISTY DAY—and in smaller letters below, LITTLE HOG ISLAND, MAINE. Before long she would return to the sea, an event Denny both anticipated and dreaded.

Marty saw her coming and immediately set up his incessant yapping, but Denny just shook her head and smiled. In a way, she was going to miss him. Mr. Jones was sitting out on the deck. He stood up and waved. Denny climbed up the ladder and perched herself on the side rail.

"What are you doing?" she asked.

"Going over some charts," he told her. He had some big, maplike things spread out on the table before him. Denny sat quietly staring out to sea while he drew lines and made notes. Funny, she thought, how she and Mr. Jones had grown comfortable with each other. They could work together for hours, talking when they felt like it, thinking their own private thoughts when they didn't. She felt a sudden heaviness and another sigh escaped from her lips. Mr. Jones looked up.

"Something wrong?" he asked.

"No," she said. "My mom might have sold her book."

"Well, that's wonderful," said Mr. Jones.

Denny nodded. "She finds out next week. If the deal goes through, we'll be moving back to New York."

Mr. Jones smiled. "Well, that's great," he said. "That's what you've wanted, isn't it?"

Denny nodded again. "Yeah," she said, and looked back out to sea.

"You don't sound all that sure," said Mr. Jones.

Denny shrugged. "Just seems like kind of a waste," she said, "to be leaving now with the summer coming and all. I never even learned to swim."

Mr. Jones looked up. "You don't swim?" he said.

105

"No," said Denny. "I never learned how."

"You don't have to learn how," said Mr. Jones. "You're born knowing how. You just have to learn not to be afraid."

"That's not so easy," said Denny.

Mr. Jones laughed. "No," he said, "learning not to be afraid is about the hardest thing any of us has to do in life."

He bent over his maps again, and Denny wondered if there was anything Mr. Jones was afraid of. After a time, the putter of an engine penetrated her thoughts and she swung her head slowly toward shore and refocused her eyes on the old red motorboat. The heaviness inside her deepened.

Denny forced a smile as Spence pulled his boat up on the black gravel beach.

"Hi!" Spence shouted as he bolted up the ladder and threw a long leg over the rail.

"Hi," Denny answered.

"Great day, isn't it?" said Spence.

"Super," said Denny.

"Denny has good news," said Mr. Jones.

"Oh?" said Spence, looking to Denny for an explanation.

"Looks like my mom's going to sell her book," said Denny.

"No kidding?" said Spence. "That's great. I've never known a real author before."

"Well," said Denny, "you won't know this one for long either. We'll be going back to New York."

Spence's smile faltered momentarily, then returned. "Oh," he said, "that's nice."

"Do you really think so?" said Denny.

"Sure," said Spence. "That's what you've wanted all along, isn't it?"

Denny turned away. "Of course," she said shortly.

Chapter 20

Denny looked up at the clock. Her mother had said she'd be home from New York by eleven. Four more hours to wait, long hours, with her future hanging in the balance; but which way did she really want the scales to tip? She just wasn't sure anymore. She went back to her term paper, but it was useless. She'd been working for hours and she hadn't even finished one page. At last she gave up and picked up a book.

Through the open window came a sound, a shout in the distance. Denny went to the screen door and listened. She didn't hear it again, but she could hear Marty yapping, not unusual, but somehow disquieting. She walked outside and down through the pines. An engine started. She came out above the bar and saw in the twilight what appeared to be Spence's boat crossing the bay back toward shore.

Odd, she thought. Spence hadn't come around since the day she'd told him she might be leaving. Why would he come over this time of night? A chilling thought came to her.

Don't be silly, she told herself. You're just mad because Spence isn't all broken up about your leaving. You know he wouldn't do anything like that.

Marty's yapping came to her again on the breeze. Why doesn't Mr. Jones put him out? she wondered. Denny wrestled with her thoughts a moment longer. Should she take a chance on disturbing Mr. Jones for nothing? If she blew the horn, he might think *she* was in trouble. On the other hand, if he *was* in some kind of trouble, and she didn't go and see, she'd never forgive herself.

Better to be safe than sorry, she decided, and hurried back to the house for the air horn. She let a blast go and waited. She could still hear Marty, but no answering shout came from Mr. Jones. She let another blast go, a longer one this time. Still no answer.

Maybe he's walking over, she thought, and she sat down to wait. No familiar form appeared on the path across the bar, and Denny's fears began to build. He couldn't be sleeping, not this early, and not with Marty yapping like that. She looked at the swirling water that surged over the bar. She judged the depth to be about four feet, but the current was strong and the water icy cold. She looked back at the house. There was no phone and no car. The only way to reach the mainland was by Mr. Jones's ship-to-shore, and that was over there, with him.

She checked her watch. Seven-thirty. Her mother wouldn't be home for three and a half more hours. She's gonna kill you for this, Denny told herself. Then she stood up, sucked in a deep breath, and stepped into the water.

Denny was unprepared for just *how* cold the water was. It penetrated her clothes and stung her whole body like icy needles. Her breath came fast and short, but she kept going, fighting the current to keep her footing. She was up to her chest and her legs were numb. She couldn't even feel her feet anymore, when suddenly she slipped on a rock and went down.

Denny panicked. The cold and the black swirled around her. There was no up, no down. She kicked wildly, trying to touch bottom again, but there was no bottom. She opened her mouth to cry out and gulped in salt water. Sputtering and choking, she thrashed about frantically, breaking through the surface just long enough to suck in a breath of air before she went under again.

You're going to die, she suddenly realized. You're going to die unless you get ahold of yourself. Slow down and think. She stopped thrashing and Mr. Jones's words came to her, clear and strong: "You're born knowing how. You just have to learn not to be afraid." Denny willed her heart to stop pounding, and she began to kick deliberately and pull at the water with her arms the way she had seen other swimmers do it. To her immense relief, her head broke through the water and she gulped another breath of air. She kept moving her arms and legs steadily, and to her amazement, she stayed afloat. She felt a momentary rush of exhilaration, until she saw how far she was from the bar. She turned and realized that if she went with the current, rather than trying to fight it, it would just bring her down the beach closer to the *Misty Day*. She relaxed as much as she could and drifted until she felt the current lessen; then she kicked and pulled in toward shore.

Denny was numb and exhausted when she finally dragged herself out on the beach, and she lay there a moment, trembling all over. She felt sick and proud and scared all in turn, and she started to cry, when suddenly Marty was beside her, yapping in her face. She looked up at him. One of his eyes was bloody, and he held his left front paw close to his chest.

"Marty, what happened?" she cried, forgetting her own misery in her sudden concern. She reached for him and he allowed her to pick him up. There was a lump over his eye, as if he'd been kicked, or hit with something, and his small foot dangled loosely as if it was broken. Denny held him tight and looked up toward the *Misty Day*, fear rising inside her.

"Mr. Jones!" she shouted, scrambling to her feet.

There was no sign of life from the boat as she struggled up the ladder, with Marty whimpering softly in her arms.

"Mr. Jones!" she called again.

There was a low moan, and Denny looked in and saw Mr. Jones's body stretched out on the cabin floor.

Chapter 21

"Mr. Jones!"

Denny put Marty down and fell on her knees beside the still form. She touched Mr. Jones's head and her hand came away wet and sticky.

"Oh, my God," she whispered. She jumped up and lit the lamp, then bent to examine Mr. Jones again. He was bleeding from a large gash on the side of his head. His breathing was quick and shallow.

"Mr. Jones," she whispered. "Mr. Jones, please answer me."

Mr. Jones did not move or open his eyes. Denny jumped up. Her eyes searched the cabin in desperation. It was torn apart, like someone had been looking for something. She ran to the ship-to-shore and switched it on. She had seen Mr. Jones use it once, and she remembered what to do. What was that word he'd told her to use in an emergency? Then she remembered.

"Mayday!" she yelled. "Mayday!"

The radio crackled and fuzzed, but finally an answer came.

"We read you," a man's voice said. "What is your position?"

"I don't know!" Denny yelled.

"Is there a landmark nearby?" the voice asked.

"Yes," said Denny, "Little Hog Island."

"What is your position relative to Little Hog Island?" the man asked.

"We're on top of it!" Denny shouted.

"Are you aground?" the man asked.

"No . . . yes . . . I don't know. Just come, and hurry, *please*," Denny cried.

"We're on our way," the man assured her.

Denny switched off the radio and ran down into the forecabin to find something to bind Mr. Jones's wound. The forecabin had been ransacked even worse than the center cabin. Denny grabbed a pillowcase and hurried back upstairs. She tore it into strips and wound the strips around Mr. Jones's head. He moaned once, but showed no other signs of consciousness.

Denny sat in the fading twilight and waited, and waited, and waited. She held Marty on her lap and comforted him. Tears ran down her cheeks.

"I hate you, Spence," she whispered. "I hate you. I hate you, and if Mr. Jones dies I will kill you."

After what seemed like forever, Denny saw lights coming across the water. She jumped up and started flicking the lamp on and off. The boat came in close to shore and hailed her with a loudspeaker.

"Did you radio a Mayday?" a man asked.

"Yes," Denny yelled. "Mr. Jones is hurt bad. Hurry."

The Coast Guard cutter lowered a small skiff into

the water, and soon welcome hands were tending to Mr. Jones.

"Is he going to be all right?" Denny kept asking.

"We hope so," was all the men would say.

While two men strapped Mr. Jones into a stretcher, a third helped Denny find a sweatsuit that belonged to Mr. Jones and made her change out of her wet things. He questioned her at length about what had happened.

The guardsmen hooked the stretcher to the dinghy hoist and lowered it over the side. Denny picked up Marty and followed. Mr. Jones moaned a few times as they carried him to the skiff, and though it hurt Denny to know he was in pain, she was glad to know that he was still alive.

"Aren't we going to the big boat?" Denny asked as the skiff swung in toward the mainland.

"The police have an ambulance waiting at the town dock," a guardsman told her. "We'll go straight there."

"Where will they take him?" Denny asked.

"There's a small hospital in Machias," the man told her. "It's not far."

"I'm going too," Denny announced.

"I think the police would rather you help them apprehend the suspect," the guardsman said. "Without your statement they can't make an arrest."

Denny's eyes narrowed, hatred for Spence once again welling up inside her.

"All right," she said. "But as soon as he's in jail, somebody has to take me to the hospital."

The guardsman nodded.

*****

The police cruiser pulled up in front of a shabby-looking house trailer that was perched on a small, overgrown lot. Denny rolled down her window and watched as the policeman, Officer Rich, knocked on the door. A tired-looking woman pulled it open.

"Evenin', Stu," she said to the policeman, a surprised look on her face.

Officer Rich tipped his hat. "Evenin', Lucy," he said. "Your boy here?"

"Somethin' wrong, Stu?" the woman asked.

"Just want to ask him a few questions."

The woman looked nervously over her shoulder. "Wilton," she called into the recesses of the trailer.

A few seconds later Spence appeared in the doorway, looking equally confused. In spite of her loathing, Denny's heart fluttered.

"Where were you about seven o'clock this evening?" Officer Rich asked Spence.

"Right here. Why?" Spence asked innocently. Denny's loathing deepened.

"Can you prove that?" asked Officer Rich.

"Of course he can," Spence's mother said. "I was here with him the whole time. He's been working on a term paper."

Denny's stomach turned. "No wonder he's a scum," she mumbled to herself. "He lies and his mother swears to it."

"I got a young lady in the cruiser," said Officer Rich,

115

"who says she saw you leaving Little Hog Island about that time."

Spence looked over the officer's shoulder.

"Denny?" he said. He came down the steps toward the car.

Denny jumped out and faced him, her chest heaving with emotion. "You liar," she shrieked. "You filthy liar. Mr. Jones may be dying, and you stand there and pretend you know nothing about it!"

Spence's eyes opened wide and his face went white. "What?" he whispered.

"You know perfectly well what!" Denny screamed. "You robbed him and beat him and left him to die!"

"Oh, no." Spence's mouth fell open and his shoulders sagged. He turned a deathly pale face to Officer Rich. "I didn't do it, Officer," he said, "but . . . but I think I know who did. I lent my boat to some guys from school. They said they wanted to go night fishing. I'll take you to them."

Denny clapped her hand over her mouth and stared at Spence's back. He turned slowly to face her again. Denny burst into tears and Spence put his arms around her and held her while she cried.

Chapter 22

Officer Rich dropped Denny and Spence at the hospital, and then left, promising to drive out to the house and leave a note for Denny's mom. Denny and Spence sat side by side in the waiting room, watching the hands of the clock creep slowly toward midnight.

Denny glanced awkwardly at Spence.

"I don't know why you don't hate me," she said.

Spence shook his head. "It's easy to understand how you got that idea. It was so stupid of me, shooting my mouth off in school like that, trying to act tough."

Denny sighed. "I'm glad it was only an act," she said. "I just hope Mr. Jones is okay."

Spence's expression darkened. "If anything happens to him," he said, "I'll kill myself."

"Don't say that," said Denny. "Although a couple of hours ago I was ready to save you the trouble."

Spence smiled. "Yeah," he said, "you looked like you could have done it too. I wouldn't want to tangle with you when you're mad."

Denny leaned back in her chair. She put her hands together and rested her chin on them. Then she glanced at Spence out of the corner of her eye and smiled.

"What's that look for?" he asked.

"Nothing," she said, giggling a little.

"Now, come on," said Spence. "You're laughing at me, and I want to know why."

Denny grinned slyly. "No reason, *Wilton.*"

Spence slugged her playfully in the arm. "Oh, yeah," he said. "Well, how about if I call you Denise?"

"There's nothing wrong with Denise."

"There's nothing wrong with Wilton either."

"Oh, no? Is that why you write W. James Spencer on all your school papers?"

"How do you know what I write on my school papers?"

Denny shrugged. "Just noticed."

"Oh, yeah?" said Spence, puffing out his chest. "What else have you noticed about me?"

Denny rolled her eyes. "That you're in love with yourself," she answered.

Spence leaned over and whispered into her ear, "Sounds like maybe I'm not the only one."

Denny blushed and turned her shoulder to Spence. "You're impossible," she whispered.

Spence leaned back and chuckled. Just then the automatic front doors of the hospital swung open and Denny's mother rushed in. Denny jumped up and ran to her arms.

"I came as soon as I saw the note," her mother said breathlessly. "You poor baby. Are you all right? I knew I shouldn't have left you alone. How's Mr. Jones?"

"I'm fine," Denny told her, "but we don't know about Mr. Jones yet."

Denny's mother shook her head. "The poor man," she said. "How long has he been in there?"

Denny looked up at the clock. "Three hours," she said. "It seems like three years."

Denny's mother sat down. "And I was so anxious to get home and tell you the good news," she said. "I thought you'd be so happy."

"You sold the book?" said Denny.

Her mother smiled and nodded.

"Oh, Mom, that's wonderful," said Denny, giving her mother another hug. "I'm really proud of you."

"Congratulations, Mrs. Townsend," said Spence.

"Thank you both," said Denny's mother. "I just wish I could be telling you under happier circumstances."

The door to the operating suite slid open and a doctor in green scrubs came out, pulling off his face mask. Denny ran over to him, and Spence and her mother jumped up and followed.

The doctor smiled. "Mr. Jones is going to be fine," he said. "We were able to stop the internal bleeding before there was any real damage. He's lucky you found him when you did."

Denny breathed a sigh of relief. "Can we see him?" she asked.

"He won't be conscious for several hours yet, and then he'll need a lot of rest," the doctor said. "Why don't you go home and get some sleep. He'll be in much better shape tomorrow."

Denny frowned but nodded.

The doctor turned to her mother. "There is one matter that concerns us," he said. "Do you know if he has any family?"

"He has a daughter," said Denny's mother.

"Do you think you could get in touch with her?"

"We can try," said Denny's mother.

"I'd appreciate that," said the doctor.

"What's the thing you're concerned about?" Denny asked.

"I'm afraid I can't discuss that with you," he told her, "but it has nothing to do with his injuries."

Denny frowned again.

"See you tomorrow," said the doctor.

There was no lawyer by the name of Andrea Jones listed in New York.

"Remember that other name?" said Denny. "The one on the photograph?"

"Yes," said Denny's mother. "Wasn't it Flannery or something like that?"

Denny shook her head. She was so tired that her mind felt all fuzzy. "I can't remember," she said.

"I can run you out there in my boat," said Spence.

"No," said Denny's mother. "it's too late. We can't call the woman this time of night anyway. We'll check in the morning."

"Please, Mom," said Denny. "It's gonna drive me crazy if I don't find out what it is. I'll be thinking about it all night."

Her mother sighed and shook her head.

"All right," she said, "but the minute you find it, Spence is to bring you straight home and walk you to the house."

Spence assured her that he would, and Denny's mother drove them to the dock and waited until they shoved off.

"She worries a lot, doesn't she?" said Spence.

"Yeah," said Denny, realizing suddenly how close she'd come that night to becoming just one more tragedy in her mother's life. "I guess she's got reason," she said quietly.

When they reached the boat, Denny lit the cabin lights.

"We've got to get this place fixed up for him before he gets back," said Spence.

Denny nodded. "He'll be all off schedule now," she said. "He was going to launch her tomorrow and get her engines hooked up by the end of the week."

"He won't lose a day," said Spence. "I'll put the word out and the townsfolk will take care of everything."

Denny looked up. "Would they do that?" she asked. "They hardly even know him."

Spence smiled. "You've got a lot to learn about down-easters," he said.

Denny pressed her lips together and nodded thoughtfully. "Yeah," she said, "maybe I do."

Spence followed her down into the forward cabin and helped her pull out a big drawer from under Mr.

Jones's bunk. "Here it is," she said. She lifted out the box of photos and started rummaging through. She found the picture she was looking for. "Fleming," she said. "That's what it was." She was about to push the box back into the drawer when another photo caught her eye. She picked it up and looked at it.

"Holy cow," she said.

"What?" said Spence.

Denny held the picture up so he could see. It was a picture of Mr. Jones taken many years ago. He was beardless and his hair was dark, and his skin was smooth and wrinkle-free. He stood on a dock, proudly holding a pole and a big string of fish. Tied up behind him, her name clearly visible, was the *Misty Day*.

Chapter 23

Denny's mother bent over the photograph. She shook her head. "I don't know what to make of it," she said. "Are you sure it's the same boat?"

"Of course," Denny insisted. "Even without the name I'd know it was the *Misty Day*."

"Then maybe it's not Mr. Jones. Maybe it's someone who looks like him."

"*Exactly* like him?" said Denny. "And if it's not Mr. Jones, why was he keeping the photograph?"

"Maybe it's his father," Spence offered.

Denny looked at the picture again, then shook her head. "No," she said. "It's him. I know it's him."

"Then he's pushing a hundred," said Spence. "It's the only explanation."

Denny's mother raised her eyebrows. "Mr. Jones? A hundred years old?" she said. "He doesn't even look like he's in his seventies."

Denny sighed, then looked at Spence. "How about that selkie business?" she asked.

Spence laughed and got up from the kitchen table. "Now you're getting crazy," he said. "Time for me to go home and get some sleep."

"That," said Denny's mother, "is the first sensible idea I've heard all night."

Denny's mother dropped her off at the store in the morning and went to pick Marty up at the vet's.

Miss Lizzie, the store owner and postmistress, nodded to her as she came in. Miss Lizzie was gray-haired and *a bit beamy*, which was a polite way the natives had of saying *plump*. She wore sleeveless housedresses and open-toed terry scuffs no matter how cold the weather, and she always smelled faintly of body odor and lavender. "Where's your mama?" Miss Lizzie asked. "She should've been in some time ago."

"We overslept," said Denny. "She'll be here soon."

Hiram Turner nodded to her from his customary perch on the lunch stool by the window. Denny had never come into the store when Hiram wasn't there smoking his cigarette and jawing to anyone who'd spend the time. He wore a red-checked hunting shirt with L. L. Bean boots and kept a black leather cap with earflaps right beside him on the counter. He always had a day's growth of stubble on his chin, never more, never less, a feat that Denny found intriguing.

"Hear you had some excitement over to the islands last night," said Hiram.

"Yeah," said Denny.

"How's the cap'n?"

"What captain?"

"Cap'n Day," said Lizzie. "That's what folks call him around town."

Denny stared at her a minute, tempted to bring up the picture, but then she thought better of the idea. The phone call was more important.

"He's going to be okay," Denny told them. "Can I use the phone?"

"It's a free country," said Lizzie, nodding toward the old pay phone on the wall.

Denny called the operator and found that there *was* an Andrea Fleming, attorney-at-law, listed in Manhattan. She dialed the number.

"You have reached the office of Andrea Fleming," a recording said. "Office hours are eight to five, but if you leave a message we will call you back as soon as possible."

Denny cleared her throat. She hated talking to machines, but she didn't have enough change to place the call again. "My name is Denise Townsend," she said, "and I need to talk to you about your father. My number is"—she looked at the old pay phone—"two oh seven, four four eight, three four eight six."

She hung up and looked at the clock: 7:37. It shouldn't be long. Denny picked up a broom and started sweeping the old floorboards, dark and soft with age.

"Hurry up with that chow," Hiram told Miss Lizzie. "I'm hungry enough to eat a boiled owl."

"Quit your blahtin', Hiram," Lizzie said, "or that's just what you'll get." She looked over at Denny. "You had any breakfast, honey?" she asked.

"I had a doughnut," Denny told her.

Miss Lizzie sniffed. "What kind of breakfast is that for a growing child?" she said. "You come over and sit down and I'll dish you up a real breakfast."

"Mom said I should sweep up," Denny said.

"This is my store and I'll decide when it needs sweeping," Miss Lizzie said. "Get on over here now."

Denny went over and sat on the stool next to Hiram. Hiram crushed out his cigarette, wolfed down his eggs and coffee, then got up and put his cap on. "Well, I'd better get to work," he said.

Lizzie snorted. "Who you kidding, Hiram?" she said. "You ain't done an honest day's work in twenty years."

"No," said Hiram, "but I'm mighty good at supavisin'."

He winked at Denny, blew Miss Lizzie a kiss, and did a sailor's hornpipe out the door.

Miss Lizzie shook her head and smiled. "Crazier than a backhouse rat," she mumbled.

"What's he going to supervise?" asked Denny.

"Bunch of the fellas are goin' over to tend to the cap'n's boat," said Lizzie.

Denny looked at her. "Why?" she asked.

Lizzie stared at her like she'd asked a very strange question. "Well, 'cause it's the neighborly thing to do, of course. Don't folks do for one another where you're from?"

Denny thought of New York, of how she'd hardly even known the people in her own apartment building, of everybody rushing—always rushing.

"I don't think they have time," she said quietly.

The phone rang and Denny jumped to answer it. "Is there a Denise Townsend there, please," a woman's voice asked nervously.

"This is Denise," said Denny.

"Denise, this is Andrea Fleming," the woman said, her voice rising in urgency. "You said something about my father. Do you know where he is?"

"Yes . . ."

"Is he all right?"

"Yes, but—"

"Oh, thank God. Where is he? Where are you calling from?"

Denny was confused. Hadn't Mr. Jones told his daughter where he was living?

"Denise? Denise, are you there?"

"Yes. I . . . I'm calling from Wellsley, Maine."

"Wellsley? Where on earth is that?"

"On the coast, up near Machias."

"Where is my father? Did he tell you to call?"

"Not exactly," said Denny. "He's in the hospital."

"The hospital! Oh, I knew it. How bad is he?"

"The doctor said he's going to be fine, but there's something he wants to talk to you about."

"I'll be on the next flight," Andrea said. "Can somebody meet me at the airport?"

"I guess so," said Denny.

"Great. I'll call you back and let you know what time. Oh . . . and thank you. You don't know what this means to me. I've been searching for my father since last fall."

Denny hung up the phone and stared at Miss Lizzie.

"Something wrong, honey?" Miss Lizzie asked.

Denny shook her head. "I don't know," she said. "I think maybe I just made a big mistake."

The door jingled and Denny's mother came in with Marty under her arm. Denny rushed over.

"Is he all right?" she asked.

Marty looked up at her and growled.

Denny's mother laughed.

Denny scowled. "I guess so," she said. "He's got his old personality back."

Chapter 24

Mrs. Townsend dropped Denny and Spence off at the hospital and then went to pick up Andrea at the airport.

"Do you think I should tell him?" Denny asked Spence.

"No," said Spence. "I think we'd just better let it be a surprise, and don't start bugging him about that picture either. He's not that strong yet."

Denny and Spence followed the nurse down a pale blue hall with gleaming floors. She pushed open a wide door with the number 36 on it.

"Company, Mr. Fleming," she said.

Denny gave Spence a quick glance, but Spence shook his head. "Play over it," he whispered.

Denny and Spence walked to the bedside. Mr. Jones's eyes were closed. His head was bandaged like a mummy's and tubes came out of his arm, connecting him to a number of bottles overhead. Wires from his chest connected him on the other side of the bed to a little television set that went *beep, beep, beep.* A line on the television set went up and down like a mountain range.

"Does that look right to you?" Denny asked Spence.

"Looks fine," said Mr. Jones abruptly. "When it goes all flat and starts whistling you got something to worry about." He opened his eyes and smiled at them.

"Mr. Jones!" said Denny. "You're okay?"

"Of course I'm okay. I've had hangovers that felt worse than this."

Denny and Spence laughed.

"Did they get those hoodlums?" Mr. Jones asked.

Spence nodded. "They got most of the money back too," he said. "All except about ten dollars."

"That's what I get for keeping my money under my mattress like an old fool," said Mr. Jones. "Is Marty okay?"

Denny smiled. "He got banged up some," she said, "but he's okay—obnoxious as ever."

Spence laughed. "Yeah," he said, "and from what the police say, the kid that he tangled with got the worse end of the deal."

Mr. Jones smiled and shook his head. A nurse walked in with some pills and a cup of water.

"I told you, I don't need that stuff," Mr. Jones told her. "What I want is a doctor so I can get out of here."

The nurse smiled and winked at Denny and Spence.

"Your friend here is a terrible patient," she said.

"I'm a terrible patient because I don't belong here. Hospitals are for sick people, and I've got work to do. Now, are you going to get me a doctor, or am I going to have to sign myself out AMA?"

"AMA?" said Denny.

"Against medical advice," the nurse explained.

Then she slapped a blood-pressure cuff on Mr. Jones and stuck a thermometer in his mouth.

"Uffoldooommmnofffick!" Mr. Jones mumbled.

"Behave yourself," the nurse told him, "or I'll order you an enema."

Mr. Jones sank back on the pillow and rolled his eyes. The nurse took the thermometer out and read it.

"The doctor will be in later," she said, winking at Denny and Spence again on her way out.

Spence started to chuckle. "I guess she told you," he said.

"Confounded hospitals," Mr. Jones mumbled. "Once they get their hands on you they never want to let you go."

"Well, you can relax," said Denny. "The folks in town are taking care of the boat and—"

"What!" said Mr. Jones, bolting up in bed. "Ow!" He grabbed his head and lay down again.

"Hangover, huh?" said Spence.

"What do you mean, taking care of the boat?" asked Mr. Jones, his eyes scrunched up in pain.

"Hiram Turner and a bunch of the guys are going to clean her up and put her in the water for you," said Denny.

Mr. Jones groaned. "It's not that I'm not appreciative," he said, "but are you sure they know what they're doing?"

Spence smiled. "Those old boys know boats better than you know your backside," he said. "They'll have her bungs up and bilge free in no time."

"Is that good?" asked Denny.

"I believe it means shipshape," said Mr. Jones.

Spence nodded.

The door to the hospital room opened a crack and Denny's mother peeked in. "Hi," she said. "Everything okay?"

"Fine," said Mr. Jones. "Come on in. Join the party."

"I've brought someone," said Denny's mother. She pushed the door open and a stylish woman with short black hair walked into the room.

Mr. Jones's mouth fell open and his face turned as white as the pillow. "Andrea . . . ," he whispered.

"Hi, Daddy."

The two stared at one another for a long time; then Mr. Jones put his arms up and his daughter rushed into them.

Chapter 25

Denny's mother put the pot back on the stove and came over and sat down next to Denny.

Andrea Fleming held her coffee cup with two hands and took a sip. "My father is . . . not well," she said.

"What do you mean, *not well*?" asked Denny. Somehow she sensed that Andrea wasn't talking about Mr. Jones's recent injuries.

Andrea sighed. "It all started after Mom died," she said. "He started talking crazy. Something about an old boat. And then a lot of nonsense that had to do with the Bermuda Triangle."

"The Bermuda Triangle?" said Denny's mother. "Isn't that some kind of mysterious place where ships and planes disappear?"

Andrea nodded. "Things like that have always fascinated my father," she said, "but after Mom died it was almost like an obsession. He kept talking about getting some old boat and going down there. He'd get all hyped up and then I'd talk him out of it, and he'd calm down for a while. Then a couple of months later he'd start in again. I never paid much attention to what he was saying. I just figured it was senility setting in, but then, when we found out about the cancer . . ."

Denny's heart thudded. "Cancer?" she said. "What cancer?"

"Last fall we discovered that Dad has bone cancer," Andrea told her. "He seemed to forget all about the boat idea, never mentioned a word. Then, the night before his surgery was scheduled he simply checked himself out of the hospital and disappeared."

"AMA?" said Denny.

"That's right," said Andrea. "How did you know?"

"He was talking about doing it again today," said Denny.

Andrea shook her head. "He won't be going anywhere this time," she said. "I've got a court order declaring him unfit and making me his guardian."

Denny winced. "Mr. Jones doesn't seem unfit," she said.

"His name is Fleming," Andrea reminded her. "Alexander Fleming, and I've had a private investigator searching boatyards all up and down the East Coast for the better part of a year. I'm not going to let him get away again."

"What are you going to do with him?" Denny's mother asked.

"As soon as he's fit, I'm going to fly him back to New York for the surgery. I just hope it's not too late."

Denny's stomach turned over. "Too late?" she asked. "What do you mean, too late?"

"The kind of cancer he has spreads very fast," Andrea told her. "If he'd had the surgery last fall and gone with the chemotherapy, he stood a chance. Now I don't know."

Denny felt her throat tightening and the sting of impending tears in her nose. She sniffed them back. "What do you mean, you don't know?" she said. "He's got to be okay."

"I hope so too," said Andrea, "but the sooner he has that surgery, the better. It would go a lot easier if he wouldn't fight it. He seems to think a lot of you. Maybe you could talk to him."

Denny stared down at the photograph she'd been holding in her hand, waiting for a chance to ask Andrea about it. Now it didn't seem to matter anymore. She rolled it up and stuffed it in her pocket.

Chapter 26

Denny met Spence in the hospital corridor. "Mr. Jones has cancer," she told him in a hushed whisper. "We've got to talk him into having an operation."

"What?" said Spence. "Who told you that?"

"His daughter. She wants to take him back to New York in a couple of days for the surgery."

"Doesn't he want to go?" asked Spence.

"No," said Denny, "and I don't know why. But we have to talk him into it. Come on."

Spence followed her into Mr. Jones's room. Mr. Jones had his eyes closed again.

"Do you think he's sleeping?" Denny whispered.

Spence shrugged.

"No," came Mr. Jones's tired reply. He opened his eyes slowly and gave them a listless smile.

"You okay?" asked Spence.

Mr. Jones nodded and closed his eyes again.

Denny and Spence gave each other a quizzical look. This wasn't the Mr. Jones they were used to.

"The launching went great yesterday," Spence offered.

"That's nice," said Mr. Jones, without moving a muscle.

"Mr. Jones," said Denny, "are you sure you're okay?"

Mr. Jones opened his eyes. "The name is Fleming," he said. "Alexander Fleming."

"Mr. Fleming," said Denny, then she hesitated. "Can I still call you Mr. Jones?" she asked. "Mr. Fleming seems like somebody else."

"Suit yourself," said Mr. Jones, closing his eyes again.

"Mr. Jones, Andrea told me about your illness."

"So, now you know everything," said Mr. Jones.

"No," said Denny. "There are still some things I don't understand."

Mr. Jones's mouth curved into a small, sad smile. "Yeah," he said. "I know. We had this conversation before." He opened his eyes again. "Well, the jig is up now," he said. "What do you want to know?"

Denny remembered the photograph, still in her pocket from last night. She pulled it out and unrolled it. "What about this?" she asked.

Mr. Jones looked at the picture and smiled. "Did you ever think about being a detective?" he asked.

Denny just shook her head and pointed to the picture.

Mr. Jones sighed. "A long time ago," he said, "maybe twenty-five years or so, I chartered a boat with some friends in the Florida Keys. The captain was an old salt, used to entertain us with some wild sea tales."

Denny's eyes opened wide. "Rufus Day?" she said.

Mr. Jones nodded. "He talked about escaping from a hurricane once by sailing straight into it. We thought he was just full of wind. He also talked about a place he was searching for, somewhere in the Bermuda Triangle, a place where a man or even a whole ship could sail through a time warp and into another dimension. He said he wasn't going to rest until he found that place. He said he and his boat were going to sail on through and just keep sailing forever. We thought he was crazy, and after I went home I never gave it another thought, until five years ago, when I came up here and happened across the same boat."

"The *Misty Day*," said Spence.

"Yes," said Mr. Jones. "It seemed like an unearthly coincidence, and when I heard the legend and found out he'd been telling the truth about the hurricane, I couldn't get it out of my mind. It was like he was calling me from somewhere, trying to tell me something. I told Martha about it, but she just pooh-poohed it and said I was talking nonsense. I tried to tell Andrea, but she thought I was getting senile. Then, when I found out about the cancer, I just couldn't put it off any longer. I had to know."

Mr. Jones got up on one elbow and looked at them both, the sparkle coming back into his eyes.

"He found it," he whispered. "It was right there on the last page of his journal—seventy-five degrees, fifty-four minutes north latitude, twenty-five degrees, forty-seven minutes west longitude."

Denny felt a shiver run up her back. "Is that in the Bermuda Triangle?" she asked.

"Yes," said Mr. Jones. "The *Misty Day* was found unmanned and adrift just off the Virginia coast, which is right where the Gulf Stream would have taken her. The date she was found, and the distance she traveled, coincide perfectly with the date of the last entry in Rufus Day's journal."

"But what could have happened to him?" asked Denny.

"I don't know," said Mr. Jones. He lay back on his pillow and his eyes grew dull again. "I guess I'll never know."

Denny and Spence looked at one another. "You meant to go down there?" said Spence.

Mr. Jones nodded.

Denny swallowed hard. "But what if it was something awful?" she said. "Weren't you scared?

Mr. Jones smiled thinly. "I guess I was scared," he said. "That's why I let Andrea talk me out of it for so long. But now I'm not scared anymore. All my life I've played it safe. You have to when you're a husband and father, and I'm not sorry. I've had a good life. But this is, or I should say was, my last chance for a great adventure."

"Don't talk like that," said Denny. "You'll be fine after your operation. You can do anything you want then."

"Yeah," said Mr. Jones. He nodded and closed his eyes again.

"You're going to have the operation then?" said Denny.

"Sure," said Mr. Jones. He rolled over and pulled his sheet up to his chin.

Chapter 27

Denny went over after school and watched Hiram Turner "supervise" the connection of the drive shafts to the engines. Mr. Jones had not shown any further interest in the *Misty Day*. He wasn't showing much interest in anything, for that matter. He seemed to be getting worse instead of better, but Andrea was taking him to New York the next day, regardless. Denny and Spence had decided to go ahead with preparing the *Misty Day* in the hope that Mr. Jones would regain his interest after the operation.

Denny heard the roar of an engine and turned to see Spence's boat speeding across the bay. She hadn't realized it could go fast. Spence never seemed to be in much of a hurry. But now he was.

"Denny!" he shouted as soon as he came alongside. "Come aboard. I've got to talk to you."

Denny threw her legs over the side of the *Misty Day* and dropped down into the smaller boat. Spence pushed off and motored out into the bay.

"What's up?" asked Denny.

Spence cut the motor down to an idle and turned to her. "We've got to get Mr. Jones out of that hospital," he said.

"What?" Denny stared at him. "Are you crazy?"

"No," said Spence. "I've been giving it a lot of thought. You've seen how he is. He's not himself."

"He's just not feeling well," said Denny.

"He's feeling fine," said Spence. "He just doesn't care anymore."

"But why?" said Denny. "Why doesn't he want the operation?"

"Do you know what the operation is?"

"What do you mean?"

"They're going to take his leg off."

Denny felt like someone had punched her in the stomach—hard. She couldn't breathe for a moment. She couldn't talk. She just stared at the bow of the boat, going up and down, up and down. "That stinks," she said at last.

"Yeah," said Spence. "That's why we've got to get him out."

"But I still don't understand," said Denny. "If it's going to save his life . . ."

"*If*," said Spence. "That's a big if. What if it doesn't work? What do they take off next? And even if it does work, how long will it be before he can sail again, if ever? He's running out of time, Den. That's what this whole thing with the *Misty Day* is really about, don't you see?"

Denny stared at him in confusion.

"It's hard to explain," Spence went on, "but it's like the *Misty Day* is really him. That's why he's so obsessed with making her new again. She was a proud ship. He's a proud man. Neither of them wants to spend the rest of their days rotting in some cradle."

Denny stared out at the sea. Spence's words angered her. She didn't want to listen anymore. "No," she said quietly. "He needs the operation. It could save his life. He's not thinking straight or he'd realize that."

"He's thinking fine," said Spence.

"He's not," said Denny, her voice rising. "You heard Andrea. She said he hasn't been right since Martha died."

"Are you trying to say he's crazy?"

Denny couldn't answer.

"Denny, look at me," said Spence. "You know he's not crazy. You know it better than anybody."

"No, I don't," said Denny. "He must be crazy not to want the operation. What about Andrea?"

"Andrea's a grown woman with a life of her own."

"So what?" said Denny. "He's still her father, and what about . . ."

"What about who, Denny? You?"

Denny looked away.

"You can't make him take your father's place, Denny. It's not fair."

Tears started down Denny's cheeks. "I'm not!" she shrieked. "Shut up! Will you just shut up?"

Spence didn't say anything more. Denny stared through her tears at the *Misty Day*, riding regally at anchor, as proud and as beautiful as the day she was made. Beyond, the sparkling blue sea beckoned. Denny closed her eyes and squeezed the tears out. She took a deep breath and turned back to Spence.

"Wilton Spencer," she said softly, "why do you have to be so damned smart?"

Spence smiled. "Darned smart," he said; then he wiped her tears away and kissed her on the tip of her nose.

Chapter 28

"So what do we do, dress up like orderlies and sneak him out in the laundry cart?"

"Something like that."

"Oh, c'mon, Spence, that routine is as old as the Three Stooges."

"Probably older," said Spence, laughing. "Actually I was thinking of something a little less dramatic."

"Like what?"

"Like just walking out with him."

Denny stared at Spence, then shook her head. "In one of the big hospitals in New York you might get away with that," she said, "but in a little tiny hospital like Down East Community, it'll never work."

"It might, if he's dressed like a woman," said Spence.

Denny thought for a minute, then nodded. "Maybe," she said. "But where are we going to get clothes to fit him? My mom and your mom are way too thin."

Spence smiled. "Miss Lizzie," he said.

Denny's eyes opened wide. "Miss Lizzie? Do you really think she'll do it?"

"She's waiting for us right now at the edge of town," said Spence. He turned the boat in and ran it up on the beach just below Denny's cottage.

"Where are we going?" asked Denny.

"To get the Jeep," said Spence.

The Jeep was parked at the edge of the causeway, just above the bar. Mr. Jones often left it there, now that he had the dinghy. The keys were always in the ignition. Mr. Jones wasn't much for security. "You only lock your friends out," he used to say. Denny wondered sadly if he'd feel differently now.

"Who's going to drive us?" Denny asked.

"I am."

"You can't drive."

"I sure can."

"How?" asked Denny. "You don't have your license yet."

"Like this," said Spence. He got into the Jeep and turned on the ignition. "Are you coming or not?"

Denny climbed in beside him. "My mother's going to kill us," she said.

Spence laughed and wheeled off down the causeway.

Miss Lizzie was waiting for them a short distance out of town. She had on the usual housedress, a baggy sweater, a plastic, higher-heeled version of the open-toed scuffs, and a big straw hat with a chiffon scarf tied around it.

"Whoowee," she said, tumbling into the backseat, "ain't this some fun? Just like in the movin' pictures."

145

"This is really nice of you, Miss Lizzie," said Denny.

"Bilge," said Miss Lizzie. "What else is a body going to do for excitement up here in the puckerbush?"

When they got to the hospital Miss Lizzie walked in just as bold as you please, making sure everyone saw her. They found Mr. Jones curled up on his side, looking shriveled and gray. The bandages were gone from his head, replaced by a small square of gauze just covering his bald spot.

"Why, it's hotter than Hades in here," said Miss Lizzie. She went right over and threw the window open. "No wonder he's lookin' so poorly. Likely he's half-cooked."

Mr. Jones opened his eyes.

"Miss Lizzie?" he said.

"Aftanoon, Cap'n," said Miss Lizzie. She gave him a wink.

Denny bent down close to Mr. Jones's face. "We're here to get you out," she whispered.

A small spark flickered in Mr. Jones's eyes.

"What?" he whispered weakly.

"We're going to help you escape," said Spence. "Do you think you're strong enough?"

Mr. Jones's eyes opened wide and a pink flush returned to his cheeks. "Are you serious?" he asked.

"Are you gonna just lay there ruminatin'?" asked Miss Lizzie, "or are you gonna get up and take that boat for a ride, now that you got her all dressed up like the deacon?"

Mr. Jones's face broke into a wide grin. The sparkle

came back to his eyes and he sat up and threw the sheets aside. "What are we waiting for?" he asked.

"Whoa, now," said Miss Lizzie. "You can't just walk out, you know. That's why I'm here." She winked again.

"You and Miss Lizzie are going to trade places," said Spence.

"Hold on," said Denny. "I just thought of something."

"What?" said Spence.

"The beard," said Denny. "We forgot about the beard."

"The heck with the beard," said Mr. Jones. "I can grow another beard. Denny, there's a razor in the packet inside that drawer over there."

Denny got the razor out of the drawer in Mr. Jones's bed tray. He took it and winked at them all. "Be right out," he said, disappearing into the bathroom.

A nurse walked into the room. "Hello," she said.

"Hello," they all answered, grinning like Cheshire cats.

"Where's Mr. Fleming?"

"Mr. Fleming?" said Denny.

"Yes, Mr. Fleming, the patient that was in that bed?"

"Oh, oh, Mr. Fleming," Denny stammered. "We, uh, call him Mr. Jones, uh, that is, he's in the bathroom."

"Oh?" said the nurse. She turned and looked at the bathroom door. "Has he been in there long?"

"Yes," said Denny.

"No," said Spence.

Miss Lizzie chuckled. "You know how it is when a body's been abed awhile," she said. "You tend to get bound up some."

The nurse went over and knocked lightly on the door.

"Mr. Fleming," she said, "do you need an enema?"

"No," came a bellow from the other side of the door, "I don't need any confounded enemas!"

The nurse came away smiling. "Sounds like he's feeling better," she said. Then she lowered her voice: "I think I'd better order that enema whether he wants it or not," she said. "I'll be back shortly."

"Terrific," said Denny after she'd gone. "Now what do we do?"

"Move fast," said Spence. "Miss Lizzie, start taking your things off. Denny, keep watch at the door."

Miss Lizzie slipped out of her sweater and pulled her housedress over her head, revealing a similar one underneath. Spence knocked on the bathroom door. Mr. Jones peeked a clean-shaven face out and Spence handed him the clothes. "Hurry," Spence whispered, "she's coming back with the enema."

Spence and Denny smothered their giggles when Mr. Jones came out of the bathroom.

"You never looked better," said Spence.

Mr. Jones smiled. "I'd put on a tutu if it'd get me out of this place," he said. "Let's go."

Miss Lizzie hopped into the bed.

"Thanks, Miss Lizzie," said Mr. Jones.

Miss Lizzie saluted. "Bon voyage, Cap'n," she said, then rolled over and pulled the sheets up to her ears.

"Cross your fingers," said Denny. "Let's go."

They pulled the door closed behind them and started nonchalantly down the hall. The nurse came bustling toward them, a big plastic bag full of water in her hand. Mr. Jones put his head down. Denny sucked in her breath. She and Mr. Jones kept walking.

"Uh, nurse?" they heard Spence say behind them.

"Yes?"

"Mr. Jones, uh, Fleming said he was really tired and wanted to sleep. Maybe you ought to wait and give him that later."

Denny heard the nurse's crisp footsteps slow. "Well," the nurse said, "I guess that'll be all right."

Denny let her breath out slowly and willed her legs not to break into a run as she and Mr. Jones neared the door. She could feel Mr. Jones's grip tighten on her arm as they walked through and nodded to the security guard. The guard nodded back.

They stepped out into the late afternoon sunshine. Mr. Jones took a deep breath. "Free at last," he whispered.

Chapter 29

"Okay, Penelope baby, do your stuff," said Mr. Jones. He turned the key to the port engine. *Vvrrrooooom!* It started right up and purred like a kitten. Mr. Jones looked at Denny. "Now for Stella," he said.

Denny crossed her fingers, closed her eyes, and said a little prayer.

Vvrrrooooom!

"*Okay*, Denny!" shouted Spence.

Denny laughed and slapped him five. Mr. Jones reached out his hand to her. She took it in her own. It was callused and worn, but powerful still. He squeezed her hand tightly. Suddenly she pulled her hand free and threw her arms around his neck just like she had at Christmas. He stiffened in the same awkward way, but he brought his arms up and hugged her back. When she looked at him there was a tear in the corner of his eye, but he quickly brushed it away.

"Got something for you," he said, "something for each of you." He went down into the forward cabin and Denny stood staring at the plaque over the doorway. "Old sailors never die," she read, then she smiled and brushed her tears away quickly before Mr. Jones returned.

"Just some stuff I don't need anymore," said Mr. Jones when he reappeared. He handed them each some rolled-up papers. Spence started to unfold his.

"Not now, not now. Open them later," said Mr. Jones. "I've got to get out of here."

Marty came limping up from the forward cabin and Denny bent to give him a farewell hug. He snarled.

"You're not fooling me one bit," Denny told him. "I know you're going to miss me like crazy."

A siren blast suddenly split the air and Denny jumped to her feet.

"Uh-oh," said Mr. Jones, his face turning pale. The harbormaster's boat was speeding across the bay.

"Get going," shouted Spence. "Come on, Denny, quick!" He dashed out of the cabin and vaulted over the side into his boat.

Denny hesitated a moment and looked up at Mr. Jones. "I love you, Pop," she whispered, kissing him quickly on the cheek; then she ran out after Spence and jumped down into his waiting arms.

"Daddy!" a voice suddenly called. "Daddy, wait, please!"

Denny and Spence turned to see Andrea waving frantically from the patrol boat. They looked up at Mr. Jones. He stood at the wheel of the *Misty Day*, his face contorted with emotion.

"Go!" Spence shouted. "What are you waiting for?"

Mr. Jones looked down at them, then over at his daughter, then his shoulders slumped and he cut his engines.

Denny and Spence looked at each other. "What's he doing?" asked Denny. Spence just shook his head.

The patrol boat came up astern of the *Misty Day*, and Denny recognized another person standing beside Andrea. It was Miss Lizzie.

"Daddy," Andrea shouted. "I was wrong. I realize that now. You have the right to live your own life. Please just let me come aboard a minute and say goodbye."

Denny and Spence looked over at Miss Lizzie. She winked and gave them the thumbs-up sign.

Chapter 30

Dear Shell,

I'm so glad you're coming while the lupines are still in bloom. Wait until you see them, all over the island, just growing wild, the most beautiful flowers, all pink and blue and lavender. I still can't believe Little Hog Island is mine now. Now and forever. I nearly died when I unrolled that piece of paper and saw that it was the deed. "Just something I don't need anymore," Mr. Jones said. I wish you could have met him, Shell. He was the neatest old guy. You should have seen him the day he left, standing tall and proud at the wheel of the Misty Day. I think that that moment alone was enough to make him happy for the rest of his life, whether he finds that place he's looking for or not. I miss him a lot, but at night when I go out on the pier and sit under the stars, it's kind of neat to know that he's out there, somewhere, doing what he's always wanted to do.

Spence got his license last week. He wants to take you for a ride in the Jeep Mr. Jones left him. He's already taken everybody in Wellsley—twice.

I can't wait for you to meet him, Shell. He's so gorgeous! Mom says fourteen is too young to be in love. What do you think? Oh, could you pick me up a bottle of Benetton perfume? I'll pay you back when you come. There are still some drawbacks to living in Maine, but mostly it's not bad. You know all those awful things I told you in the beginning? Well, I guess you could say I exaggerated a little. . . .